A Highball and a Low Blow

by

Constance Barker

Sign up for Constance Barker's New Releases Newsletter

Chapter One

Some little girls dream of becoming a veterinarian, doctor, or nurse. For a little while when I was five or six, I may have fantasized about becoming a princess and maybe even owned a frilly, pink costume dress. But living in Potter's Mill, a small southern town about forty-five minutes from Savannah, that quickly passed. Several of my friends grew up while helping their parents with crops and animals; I helped mine run a pub. It was just the way it was since the business has been in my family for one hundred and fifty years. I was destined to be the next owner. And that is fine by me. The Grumpy Chicken is home and has provided me many friends and fond memories.

I should mention the rumors that the pub is haunted by an ornery bird, our namesake grumpy chicken. When young, I resented hearing stories of the said feathery ghost since we lived in an apartment over the pub. The possibility of sharing our home with a poltergeist spooked me as a little girl. But now as an adult who manages The Grumpy Chicken, I endure debates with my father on how to market our alleged haunted drinking and dining establishment. I wish my mom was still alive to help me gently deal with some of Dad's more far-fetched promotion ideas.

"Ginger, what about this? You know how they do dinner shows in the city? The ones where you need to help solve a crime or something. We can offer dinner and a seance. This pretty lady here can try to make contact with the grumper after we serve up a nice dinner to the crowd." Dad put his arm around Star, our town medium, and shook her softly.

We just finished with serving the lunch rush and were sitting at a table in the dining room enjoying a drink with Star, the owner of the new age shop next door to us. I twirled the ice in my tea and laid the teaspoon on the table. "Dad, I think your ideas are always interesting. But we're a simple Irish pub and trying to contact a chicken ghost is kind of...weird. And the last few months since The Ghost Hounds were here have been *really* busy. We don't need to worry about drumming up business."

"Yeah, but how long will the boost we got from that silly TV show keep the people coming in? We can use the ol' grumper to get new customers interested."

"We barely keep up with the crowds now, even with adding Becca to wait tables part-time. If the business starts to fall off, then we can talk about some marketing ideas. But for now, I'm struggling to keep the place stocked and the customers happy."

"Sweetie, you're missing the big picture here. The sky's the limit!"

"I know you think big, Dad, but right now we need to get back to work." I love my father, but his recent obsession with marketing our alleged chicken spirit was draining. "We're just simple pub owners and we need to focus on keeping the beer flowing and the food edible."

Star took a deep breath. "Ginger, we've made some good money from the merchandise your Dad and I sell at the new age shop. We could use some of that money to buy props and dress up the dining room for the event. I think it would be fun." Star smiled and raised her eyebrows instead of asking what I thought.

I sighed. "I know you two love this, but it's not my cup of tea."

Dixie wiped the bar surface as she shouted over to us. "Hey! Is the iced tea council of Trent done yet? You going to ever get back to work?"

Dad responded. "Hey, yourself! I'm the boss. Is that any way to talk to me?"

"I've said far worse to you, old-timer, and you know it." Dixie smiled at Dad and he returned it. She continued, "Well? You know I'm right. We've citrus to cut, food to prep, kegs to swap out, dishes to wash..."

Bones shouted from the kitchen. "I'm washing the dishes. I got that one."

Dixie finished. "...And we didn't get our liquor delivery."

I banged my hand on the table. "Again! That's becoming a problem."

Dixie came over and sat down with us. "Ginger, maybe you should talk to Jacob. I know you're loyal to our suppliers, but I need to have full bottles of liquor on the shelf or we don't sell drinks. Simple as that."

I eyed her for a moment. "How do I put this politely? I have reservations about my cheating ex-husband becoming a supplier for us."

Dad added, "I don't like it at all. Never liked that English lad."

I turned to Dad. "Look, business is business. So I think we just need to go over to the general store and see Freddie Warner. Talk to him. If he can't keep us supplied, then *maybe* I'll take a call from Jacob. Lord knows he calls every week." I took a sip of my iced tea.

Dixie plopped against the back of her chair and folded her arms. "Bull snots! You know Freddie can't keep us stocked. He's just a general store and is used to selling a case of wine at the most. Since the TV show was here, we're going through cases of hard liquor and a number of kegs every week. We need a real distributor supplying us now. And in this area, your ex just happens to be the sales rep for booze."

Star tilted her head to one side. "Ginger, how long

have you been divorced now?"

I twirled my spoon again. "Almost four years. You know that."

Star nodded. "That's what I thought, but I wasn't sure. Do you still have feelings for him?"

Dad huffed. "She better not, that no good son of a..."

"Dad, stop. We all know you don't like him and it's of no use to put your cash in the swear jar over him."

Dad grumbled. "I can't believe I can't cuss in my own pub."

I laughed. "It's a family place, Dad, and your rule. You put it in place to control Dixie. Remember?"

Dad folded his arms. "Yeah, I remember. Does bull snots count?"

Dixie and I replied together. "No."

Star shuffled in her seat. "Soooooo, when you're ready to conduct a seance, I can do it on pretty short notice. Let me know." She stood. "I need to get back to work. I don't like leaving the store closed for too long. I need to get back in case someone just wants to pop in for a reading. Thanks for the iced tea and bye for now." Star waved at us as she started for the exit.

While walking toward the front door, Star stopped and put a hand to her temple for a moment, then turned back to us. "Ginger, it's kind of strange, but something is telling me Jacob will call you today." Star looked at the ground and shuddered. "And it's important you speak with him."

I stood and went over to put my arm around her. "Are you alright? You look a little white."

Star smiled. "All in a days work for a medium."

Dixie snorted. "Well, glad I'm not a medium then. That looks like it hurt."

Star rubbed her eyes. "It doesn't hurt. But sometimes I get a little dizzy, or even nauseous."

Dixie chuckled. "Maybe it's more like my job than I thought. I get dizzy and nauseous all the time putting up with the regulars in here."

I glared at Dixie then helped Star sit again. That was when the phone at the bar rang. Dixie rose from her seat and went to answer. She spoke to the caller for a few seconds then held up the old-fashioned handset of the land line phone with her hand over the mouthpiece. "Ginger, you're not going to believe this. It's Jacob."

I pinched my lips. "Bull snots!"

Star looked up at me. "See, I told you. And you need to talk to him."

"So I guess I should take this call then." I walked over to the bar.

Dixie held out the receiver. "You're stealing my non-swear cuss words now. Do I need to copyright them?"

I grabbed the phone from her. "What should I have said, 'bull boogers?' Would that have made you happy?" Dixie shrugged and I put the handset to ear. "Hello, Jacob?"

"Yeah, it's me. It's been a while but it's good to hear your voice." His voice sounded tired but I recognized it right off.

"Okay, I guess? Look, I don't mean to be rude, but you've been calling here, *a lot*. Why?"

"Well, I can tell you're not enthused to hear from me. I understand. But please allow me to just say I'm glad you took my call. And as for why I called, you may or may not know I'm the sales rep in this area selling bulk beer and liquor for a regional distributor out of Savannah. I saw you on TV and hear you're doing a ton of business. So I may have some good deals you'll be interested in."

"Well, it just so happens that the general store is having problems keeping us stocked. You might be calling at the right time."

"Who do you think stocks Freddie over at the general store? We do, through another middleman that just drives your costs up. I can save you some money."

"Okay. So can we do this over the phone?"

"I guess we could, but face to face is better. And I'm

passing by there later this afternoon. I could be there at four. Can you meet?"

I sighed. "Yeah, in the bar. I'm pretty busy, but can take a few minutes with Dixie to meet with you. So four it is."

I hung up and looked over at Dixie. The grin on her face made the Cheshire Cat look like it was scowling. "Well?"

"Well, you got a meeting with me at four o'clock. I'm not meeting with him alone. So, draft up the order we need filled for liquor and beer, if you haven't already. Jacob will be here then and we need to talk to him about possibly selling to us."

Dixie tilted her head back a little. "Well, you don't have to be so grouchy about it."

"What? I prefer to think I'm tough, not grouchy. And I just want my pub stocked properly, with no drama."

She laughed. "That's you I guess. Ms. Ginger O'Mallory, the no drama but grouchy, I mean tough, businesswoman."

"That's nice. Did you get it all out? Now, I need you to get me what you think we need before four, let's say by three, so we can be prepared to meet Jacob."

Dixie looked at the clock over the bar. "That's twenty minutes from now."

"Yes, it is. You better hurry."

She wiped a glass, slowly. "I have the list already and we can go over it now if you want. So, ya gonna freshen up. You know, put some makeup on, or something?"

I glared at Dixie. "It's not like that. I have no interest in impressing him."

"Sorry, not trying to be nosy." And with that, I decided this particular discussion was over.

We went to work and four o'clock came fast. Jacob was right on time and all business. He was dressed in a nicely pressed light blue shirt and dark trousers. His black hair was neatly cut and combed. And at his side, he carried an expensive looking leather messenger bag. My ex-husband entered through the front door like he owned the place until an odd sound emanating from every direction within the pub greeted Jacob. Everyone froze. It was hard to describe the noise but the place went quiet. Then it came again. "WHAAAACK!" "WHAAAACK!"

Dixie's jaw hung and after a few moments, she broke the silence. "Psycho Fido! That sounded like our grumpy chicken trying to impersonate a dog barking at a squirrel."

I sputtered. "Think about that sentence and how silly it sounds. It's just the building creaking."

Dixie looked around. "I never heard anything creak like that before! If that's the building then we need a contractor stat! It was the Chicken and was barking at Jacob."

I saw Jacob was also looking around and I went over to greet him. I offered my hand for a shake. "I see you still know how to find the place."

"Yeah, and I see The Grumpy Chicken is still full of surprises. What was that noise?"

I scanned the ceiling. "It's just the place creaking. We hear all kinds of weird sounds coming from this old building."

Dad walked over and faced Jacob. "You do anything to hurt Ginger, I swear...'

Jacob waved his hand. "No, this is just business. Yes, it's good to be back here and see you all. But nothing more."

Dad eyed him. "Do your business and leave us be." Dad walked off.

I intercepted the conversation. I needed to keep this professional. "Sorry about Dad. But, you know how he gets!"

Jacob smiled. "As always. Ginger coming to the rescue."

"So come have a seat at the bar and we can talk about our liquor and beer needs."

"Thanks."

We grabbed stools at the end of the bar and finished the pleasantries. Dixie then produced the order we wanted filled and Jacob scanned it. "I can get you all of this, by tomorrow. If we sign the papers today."

"I would appreciate the fast delivery. I guess that's the advantage of a full warehouse only forty-five minutes away. But let's talk price."

Jacob scribbled a few notes and referenced his phone a couple of times to look things up. Then he totaled the list and showed me the price. I picked it up and reviewed the quote. "I have to admit, Jacob. You were a no good, lying, cheating spouse, but this is a good price. There might be some hope for you as a salesman."

He smiled. "I'm a great salesman. And since I'm already here, we can sign the contract and expedite your order. You'll have it tomorrow, just like you wanted."

"Okay, let's do it. I need my pub stocked."

Dad watched us closely from a distance then went out of his way to walk by us and huffed, glaring at Jacob the whole time. "What have we come to? Doing business with this no good..."

Jacob smiled back at Dad. "Just making sure you have beer on tap."

Dad growled. "My taps have never run dry. That's bad business for an Irish pub."

Jacob nodded. "Precisely! And I saved you some

money in the process." Dad looked down his nose at my ex-husband and then stormed away. Jacob turned to me. "So, do they still serve the best chicken fried steak at Grandma's Diner?"

"Yeah, they do. But you gotta call Mable ahead to see if she's open. She only works when she feels like it."

"Care to join me?"

Dixie sat up straight like she was pinched. I eyed Jacob for a moment before answering. "You can't be serious. I'm pretty busy here and will have to pass on your offer."

"Shame. I would have loved to catch up some more. Hear all about your appearance on that TV show."

"Yeah, but I have responsibilities here to take care of. But I can call Mable at the diner to see if she is open."

Jacob smoothed his shirt and put away the binder he had taken out of his bag. "That's alright. I called Dottie and booked a room over at The Fluffy Pillow. She can help me find a hot meal. It was good to see y'all and thanks for the order."

I smiled at him for the first time. "You're welcome. And thanks for coming by, helping us get this order taken care of. See ya around I guess."

"Of course, I'm your number one liquor salesman now." Jacob was right. It happened fast and he was our new supplier of adult drinks, a key component to running an Irish pub.

Chapter Two

The next morning I was in the kitchen early getting ready for another busy day. I saw the empty kegs stacked at the rear door and was relieved a liquor delivery was set for today. We were almost out. Around eight thirty, my cell phone rang and I picked up without even looking at who it was. "Hello?"

"Ginger, it's Kelly."

"Sheriff? It's kind of early for you to be calling, what can I do for you? Is Aunt Mae alright?"

"Mae is fine. Listen, I need you to come on down to the station for a chat. Something has happened I need to talk to you about."

"What's going on?"

"It's better if you come on down and we can talk about it here."

"I guess I can be there in twenty."

"Great. I'll see you then." He clicked off.

I finished what I was doing and made some arrangements with Dad to cover everything while I was gone. I left and made the walk over, arriving at the police station to spot a state police car parked out front. This was not a good sign. The state troopers worked with our local department every now and then, and it was always when something awful happened.

I slowly opened the glass door and Eunice saw me entering. "Ginger, so nice to see you. Sheriff Morrison is expecting you. He's in the conference room." She pointed down the hall.

"Thanks, Eunice." I knew the way and made the short walk.

As I entered the room, I saw two uniformed state troopers and another man in street clothes. I was pretty sure he was a plainclothes detective. "Good morning, Sheriff. It's pretty crowded in here. What can I do for ya?"

Sheriff Morrison pointed to a chair. "Have a seat Ginger."

"Sure."

The Sheriff smiled at me. "Thanks for coming on short notice."

"Always glad to help." I sat as I spoke.

One of the state troopers leaned forward. "Kelly here, I should say, Sheriff Morrison said you would be happy to try and help us. Thank you for coming down. We know you met with your ex-husband, Jacob Allen, yesterday. Could you tell us how long it has been since you saw him last?"

"A couple of years maybe."

The trooper continued. "So why did he show up now? And was he alone?"

"Yes, he was alone. And he stopped by to sell me liquor and beer. He's the local sales rep."

The trooper made some notes. "How long did you meet with him?"

"I don't know. Not long. Twenty, twenty-five minutes."

"Did you go to dinner with him, or have drinks last night?"

"No. He invited me, but I declined. He said he was going to Grandma's Diner for some chicken fried steak."

"Do you know if he was meeting anyone?"

I glanced over at Kelly. "Look, Sheriff, I'm not sure what's going on here, but I know enough. What's happened with Jacob? Is he alright?"

The Sheriff paused. "No. He's in the hospital, in a coma."

I gasped. "What happened? Is he expected to recover?"

The Sheriff dropped his eyes. "We're not sure. He had some bad burns on his right hand and was unconscious when some of the other guests from the B&B found him in his car. Early this morning just after sunrise."

"Oh my God! What's going on? How could this happen?"

The second state trooper. answered. "I understand you were once married to Jacob and now you're worried about him. We get it. But Sheriff Morrison told you everything we know about his condition right now. Now we need to ask *you* the questions, not the other way around. So, could you please tell us if Jacob was meeting anyone else?"

I paused. "No. I don't think so."

"Are you sure?"

"Yes. Just like you told me all you know, I've told you all I know."

Sheriff Morrison jumped in. "Ginger, I know this is hard. If you could help us in any way, we would appreciate it. And if you think of anything, please let us know."

"I always assist the police whenever I can. You know that. This time is no different. But that's all I know. Can I go now?"

"Thanks, Ginger." The Sheriff looked at the other men and they nodded back to him. "You can go. Thanks again for your time."

"Anytime Sheriff. Glad to help."

I left the station a little jolted. This was an unexpected problem for me. I sat on the bench out front of the station to think, my head hung low. After a couple of minutes, Aunt Mae took a seat next to me. "Ginger, are you okay?"

I didn't move. "No. I can't figure out what happened. I see my ex-husband for the first time in a couple of years and he turns up in the hospital."

"The police can't figure that one out either. It's odd for sure. But the Sheriff and I know you had nothing to do with it."

I stared at her. "I really didn't. I just wanted my bar stocked with drinks."

"I know, dear. I feel so bad for you. I knew it would be a shock and I'm not surprised I found you sitting here trying to sort things out."

"I was thinking, yes, but I sure haven't sorted anything out. I need to know what happened, and why. How did Jacob get put into a coma? And what about the burns on his hand? That's what they told me. He had burns on his right hand."

Aunt Mae pursed her lips a bit. "Sweetie. We're not sure, still. But we're inspecting his car. It appears that he may have been shocked when he tried to start it up."

I picked my head up. "Was Jacob still driving that old Mustang?"

"Yeah, he was."

"He loved that old car, I'm not surprised. But that would mean he would have to use an old-fashioned key to start it with his right hand."

Aunt Mae smiled, a little. "Such a beautiful girl and twice as smart as you are pretty. We're pretty sure Jacob got an electrical shock when he turned the key. But we don't know why."

"The state trooper's demeanor makes more sense now. They clearly think someone tried to hurt or kill Jacob. It's not normal for a car to shock someone when starting the engine. So it's more likely someone rigged the car to electrocute him."

"Sure. That's what I think everyone is assuming right now. Until we learn what the tech's find on the car."

"When will you know something about the car inspection then?"

"Probably later today."

"Well, I'm guessing they'll find someone messed with the car. Rigged it to shock him. So then the questions are who did it and why."

Mae nodded. "Yep."

"And if I was in a pair of police shoes, I would focus on me as one of the prime suspects."

"That's true, too, sweetheart." Aunt Mae put her arm

around me. "You know I will help you any way I can, right?"

"I do and thank you. And you know this means I need to find out what happened to Jacob. Right?"

Aunt Mae chuckled. "I would expect no less of you, honey."

Chapter Three

I returned to The Grumpy Chicken to find Dixie arguing with Bones. "I've seen far more things in here than you. Trust me, it *was* the grumpy chicken barking at Jacob."

Bones dumped some ice into a cooler. "I don't know, back in the kitchen it sounded pretty muffled to me. And a chicken trying to bark like a dog, that's silly. Maybe Ginger was right, it was just the building creaking."

Dixie spotted me coming over. "The ignorance of youth. He thinks it was the building creaking. Can you believe it? Wait, who am I asking? Ms. it's the building creaking herself."

I plopped on a stool and leaned on the bar. "Dixie, I don't mean to be rude. But I have other things on my mind right now."

Bones looked at me sideways. "Uh oh, I don't like that tone, boss. I've heard it before and it means bad news."

I smiled at him. "You're becoming more observant, Bones. You're right, something bad happened. Jacob is in the hospital, in a coma. The police aren't sure why, but someone may have tried to hurt or kill him. And we were one of the last places he visited yesterday. Sooooo, the police just asked me a bunch of questions." I sighed.

"I don't like being a potential suspect."

Dixie snorted. "Great! You know what that mean's Bones? We are going to be working alone, *again*! Well, at least this time we have Becca to help us with the last half of the workday."

Dad was in the kitchen and he came through the swinging door out into the dining room. He spotted me sitting at the bar talking to Dixie. "Well, about time you got back. What did the police want?"

"Dad, come sit with me. Things are a little complicated."

Dad huffed. "I hate complicated. But anything for my little girl."

After making a production of it, he finally sat on the stool next to me and I used my calm voice. "Dad, Jacob was hurt early this morning. And the police think it's odd that after two years of no contact, Jacob meets with me then turns up in a coma at the hospital."

"That's absurd. And they should be more concerned about me. I don't like him. Never will!"

"We all know you don't like him and it's sweet you worry about me like that." I touched his hand. "But, Dad, this is serious. I may have to take some time and find out who tried to hurt him, and why."

Dad huffed. "I think you should just leave this one to the police. I don't want you getting hurt over him. It's not worth it."

"I won't get hurt. I'm a big girl now and can take care of myself."

Dad sighed. "I know you can. But it's hard for a father to see his young daughter grow into a woman. And I'll never be able to think clearly when men are involved in your life. You remember when you were in high school? That time when I took that young football player by the scruff of the neck and showed him the door for putting his arm around you? Right in front of me, too!"

"He was the star linebacker and captain of the team. How could I forget?"

"I tend to be protective, I guess. I'm sorry."

"It's okay. I understand it's because you love me, Dad. But back in high school, that boy's parents were just a tad upset with us. And I almost got kicked off the cheer leading team. I remember that part too."

"I didn't hurt him. He was fine and more important he got the message. Respect my little girl and her family, that's all I wanted."

"Yes, he got a message, but maybe not exactly the one you intended. And as usual, Mom needed to talk with his family to restore the peace. Plus, I had to promise not to date any more football players if I wanted to stay on the cheer squad."

"It was always your Mom that smoothed things over when it came to your boyfriends. She seemed to have a knack for making things right. I miss her so much."

"I miss Mom, too, every day." My mother passed while I was going through the divorce from Jacob. That was a dark time in my life and talking about her cut deeper than I anticipated. Her loss created a void in my life and I could use some of her wisdom right about now. I needed to know who would hurt Jacob and why. But I was uncertain what to do next. I rubbed my eyes and then plunked my hands on the bar. "I could use some fresh air. You got things covered fine here without me. I'll be back in an hour or two." I rose and made for the front door.

I headed down Potter's Alley, toward the old hilltop church. The one that sits across from the old Civil War cemetery. But my intended spot was the more modern cemetery, the one next to the church where Mom was buried.

The walk allowed me some time to think. I couldn't help but go back to the day Mom died. She was working in The Grumpy Chicken and everything seemed to be fine. And then she clutched her chest and fell to the floor. She died in the ambulance. Several doctors were involved and they attempted to explain the sudden heart stoppage. Some called it a heart attack, while others said that was not accurate because her heart just stopped. One doctor even said the stoppage was rare but happened when someone is shocked or frightened suddenly. I finally decided to ignore all the chatter from the doctors. It did not bring my mother back to life.

But the most mysterious part of that day was something that failed to occur. When I was growing up, Mom would often start to tell me something, seemingly important, then stop and say I was not old enough yet. The day before she died she was going to tell me, but I was too busy to listen. I told her to tell me the next day. But that was the day she died. The mystery ate at me and I frequently tried to figure it out, but I remain clueless as to what she wanted to share with me. I even asked Dad a number of times, but he has no idea what I am talking about. To this day, I still feel like a failure because the mystery remains unsolved.

It took about thirty minutes to get to the cemetery and the exercise helped. I arrived at Mom's grave site and sat on the grass at the foot of her well-groomed plot. "Mom, Dad and I miss you so much. I could use some of your insight and strength today. It's not even noon yet, and it's already been a long day. Someone hurt Jacob, put him in a coma, and the police think I'm a suspect. Why do these things keep happening to me?"

The answer to my question came from behind me. "Fate has a way of throwing things at us sometimes with no hint it's coming." Digger was dirty and brushing off his overalls. I forgot he might be working. He studied Mom's resting place. "I make sure the grass is always cut for her and clean the stone at least twice a week. We all miss her. She was a good person."

"I feel so silly, I didn't see you there. And thanks for

taking such good care of her. Her spot always looks so nice."

"You're welcome. I could tell you were talking to her but didn't quite make out what you were saying. But Ginger, I'm part of the flatfoot gang, or whatever we're calling it now. And I know when something has happened. You can talk to me. I'm here for you, except if cats are involved." He smiled at his self-deprivation.

I smiled back at him. "No cats. But my ex-husband is in the hospital, in a coma, after meeting with me only a few hours earlier. The state police think I'm a potential suspect."

"Ouch! What's with you O'Mallorys? You own a haunted pub and seem to be a magnet for drama."

"I know. Look, I'm not trying to be bad-mannered, but you got work to do and I was hoping to be alone with Mom for a bit."

Digger smiled. "I understand. I'm working over there a ways. Let me know if you need something, or want to talk." He pointed to a nearby spot.

"Thanks, Digger. That's real nice of you."

Digger went back to work and I pondered how I could be so lucky and unlucky, all at the same time. He was right, strange things happened to me far too often lately, and maybe fate was making sure I had enough bad luck to stay on my toes. But I was also luckier than most to have so many caring friends and family around me. I leaned forward to remove some small sticks and pebbles from the lawn covering Mom. A tear managed to sneak out and rolled down my cheek. I brushed it away.

"Mom, you remember that time when I was a little girl and Piper was my best friend; when we saved up our pennies? It took some time, but we managed to get enough to chip in together and buy a Game Boy. We wanted one so bad and were ecstatic the day we got it. But we had to share it and the first night didn't go well. Someone got to keep it with them while they slept. I was angry and upset because Piper won the coin toss. You knew and talked to me while tucking me into bed. Then you told me something I will always cherish. You said 'Ginger, sweetie. I know you're only nine years old. So it might be hard to understand, but when you get older you'll realize friends and family are far more important than things like a Game Boy. Friends are more important than any toy, or even things like money or gold. The most precious thing in life is the people we love. Without loved ones, you are truly poor.' You were so right, Mom."

By her definition I was rich, even after losing her. My life was full of friends and family that loved me. And this visit with Mom made me realize that I loved them even more than I thought. Mom was still teaching me life lessons.

"Ginger, you're so predictable." Dad was breathing heavy as he made the walk over to me. I started to rise to go help him, but he waved his hand at me. "No, stay there. I want to visit her, too." It took a minute for him to make it over. "This is the first time you've been here in a while. I was worried about you."

"I know. But today seemed like a good time to chat with her."

"What did you talk about?"

"You remember that Game Boy fight I had with Piper?"

"How could I forget? I was so proud of you."

"You were proud of me? Why?

"First, you saved up enough to by that expensive little gizmo. When you wanted something, you made it happen. Still do. And second, when you fought over who should keep the toy overnight, you learned friends and family are the real important things in life, not some possession. It was one of the many times I realized how special you are." He sat next to me and gave me a hug.

"For an old coot, you're pretty observant. And now that I know your memory is actually pretty good, don't pull that 'I'm old and can't remember' crap with me ever again."

"Some things I'll never forget. And that was one of those times, sweetie." Dad looked at the small headstone. "I wish I could have afforded one of those big granite markers. You know the ones that stand eight feet tall like a church steeple? She deserves it."

"I think Mom would forego a big piece of granite to have us here together like this, as a family. That's all she ever really wanted."

"You may be right. And to be honest, it's all I really want, too." Dad wiped his nose and sniffled. "So, what are you going to do now?"

"Things move too slow when the state troopers get involved. And outsiders never understand our small town nuances, even if it is the state police. So, I'm not sure of how I'm going to do it, but I need to find out who wanted to kill Jacob, and why. Speed up the process and make sure this doesn't get out of hand for any of us. Especially me. I'm sure the state police think I'm the prime suspect and I can't have that."

"That's my girl. Me and Dixie can run the pub while you help the police sort this out."

"Thanks, Dad." I kissed him on the cheek and we sat there, quiet, to take in the calm beauty of this special place.

Chapter Four

Dad and I walked back to the pub after our time with Mom and both of us were feeling a little better. My head was a clearer and I felt a new sense of purpose.

On arriving home, the first to-do-list item was call Piper Freeman and Ida Bell. Piper's journalist's skills were valuable when investigating suspicious events, like the odd electrocution of Jacob. And Ida could use a computer to find out just about anything, which was handy even if her methods fall into the gray area of the law sometimes. Between the three of us, I was confident we would find what Jacob was caught up in and who might have wanted him dead. Law enforcement does a fine job, but when the state police get involved things drag on too much and I couldn't waste much time being a suspect. It was stressful and I hated it, but it might also be bad for my reputation. Even worse it could taint the perception of The Grumpy Chicken. I needed to solve this fast and any help we could give the police would speed a resolution.

I called them both and explained what happened then asked Piper and Ida to meet me in the apartment above the bar. I was uncertain of the next steps or what was going on with Jacob, so it was better to keep my intentions concealed for now. If the rest of the gang found out they would insist on being involved, but for now, that was not necessary and would just complicate things.

Piper was the first to show while I made some coffee. She mindlessly chatted as we waited for Ida. "Ginger, you ever think about moving out of here. This apartment is so tiny."

I cleaned some spilled coffee grounds from the counter top. "Well, I was never a big city journalist like you and never experienced life in the penthouse."

Piper shot back. "I lived in an apartment smaller than this when I worked in Atlanta." She paused and her expression changed. "I get your point, sorry. I know you grew up here and it will always be your home. I was just making small talk."

"I know. Where's Ida? We should start without her. I think the first step is to have Ida dig up the various business and personal dealings Jacob had over the last year."

"If she can go back a couple of years, that's even better."

"That's the first step. And then what? What else do we do?"

Piper closed her eyes for a moment, then they popped open. "Hey, didn't you say he works out of Savannah now? We should make a road trip to check out where he lives and works. See what we can dig up."

"That's a good idea."

There was a knock at the door, finally, and I let Ida in.

She was on her cell phone. "Scooter, I'm at Ginger's and need to go. I can call you back later, okay? Bye for now. Love you." She was beaming as she clicked off.

Piper suppressed a grin. "So, sounds like the long-distance relationship with your hunky cameraman is still hot and steamy."

Ida studied Piper for a tick. "Well and hello to you, too. Sounds like you're jealous."

"No!" Piper glared back.

I rolled my eyes. "Ladies, please!"

Ida put her phone in her pocket. "Sorry. Hey, so can I have some of that coffee?"

I poured her a cup. "Sure, glad you decided to join us."

Ida shrugged. "Of course. I always want to help my friends."

"Alright. So we were talking and think you should set up the hack shack again to look into Jacob's background. But not in the pub's office. It's too visible. Can we set it up here in the apartment?"

Ida nodded. "I can set it up wherever you want. But it makes more sense for me to just work out of my place. Why move all the computers and it's easier to keep out of sight that way."

"That's a great idea and thanks for offering. I want to

keep this quiet, so please check on the last two years of Jacob's life, discreetly. I'm not sure who or what we are looking for. But it's something important enough to hurt or kill him."

Ida chuckled. "Well, that's vague. But I like a challenge."

I sighed. "After that, I'm not sure. Piper thinks we should visit Savannah and see what we can dig up at his home and workplace. That may be a good idea. But what else?"

Ida cleared her throat. "I was thinking after you called and told me what happened that I really want a look at Jacob's car. See what was used to try and electrocute him. That might give us a clue on who or what we're looking for."

"Aunt Mae said the state techs are looking the car over. I can find out what they learn from her."

Piper added, "I can also head over to The Fluffy Pillow and ask Dottie a few questions about Jacob's stay. Maybe she saw or knows something that will help."

I looked her square in the eye. "Be discreet. We don't want anyone knowing we're investigating this. Dottie has helped us before, so she can be trusted. But keep it hush-hush."

"I understand, low profile. No throwing rocks through the windows."

Ida laughed. "Dog Breath is not good under pressure. I'll never understand why he threw a rock that day."

I ignored Ida and took a deep breath. "So we all have things to do. Is there anything else you can think of?"

Ida raised her hand like a schoolgirl. "It's a little early for dinner, but I'm hungry. What's the special today?"

"Are you serious? Blue cheeseburgers."

Ida scrunched her face like she was in pain. "Can I get a plate to go? I like to eat while I'm working."

"I guess. Wait a minute, we should all have a bite in the pub. People know Jacob was hurt this morning and we can't ignore it or just disappear. Everyone would know we're poking around. So we should spend time in the pub getting a bite to eat where everyone can see us."

Piper shrugged. "I could eat now."

So we headed down to The Grumpy Chicken and took a seat at the table next to Potter's Mill's spinster sisters. Edith lit up when she saw us. "Ginger! So nice to see you. Were your ears ringing? We were just talking about what happened to Jacob. It's just awful."

"Yes, it is. I am hoping he comes out of the coma soon and fully recovers."

Lily replied. "That is noble of you, considering how much of a louse he was to you."

"After cheating on me, I have few good things to say

about my ex as a husband. But he's a human being and I would never wish him ill."

Lily grinned and leaned slightly in my direction. "Not even a little?"

Guardrail saved me. He came over holding a mug of beer in his huge fist with Dog Breath in tow. "Ginger, where have you been. Everyone was worried about you."

I smiled at the big guy. "Thanks, Guardrail. That's nice of you to worry."

Dog spoke as he sat with Lily and Edith. "Well, we're worried, yes. But worried you're investigating this without us."

Ida laughed. "Well, that killed a tender moment. Thanks, Dog. At least you're honest."

Dog shrugged. "I'm always honest and to the point."

Guardrail waved off Dog then looked at me. "We all know that the police questioned you today. And Digger told us he saw you down at your Mom's grave. So we all came on over to offer help. But you weren't here and we were concerned."

"Thanks. I spent some time down at the cemetery chatting with Mom. Then Ida and Piper came over to the apartment to talk over some coffee. Seeing Jacob brought back a tough time in my life and I was just stepping back a bit to relax, unwind. I appreciate your concern and friendship more than you know."

Dixie came over with Dad and they stood next to Guardrail. Dixie nudged Tom. "See, I told you they would get the gang together. Help keep Ginger from being dragged into this as a suspect. The police are good, but they move too slow."

I raised my voice. "No. That's not it Dixie. We're all just talking. We were hungry and just wanted some dinner, so it's just coincidence. But it's a good chance to catch up since we're all here together."

Back at the bar, Digger finished his burger and eventually left his dinner plate to came over to us. "Not a coincidence at all. We're here to help." He sat at my table. "We know your Mom's death hit you hard. And it happened during the divorce. It was the only time I ever saw you rattled. Then you turn up today at the cemetery after Jacob is hurt. It's not hard to guess you're upset."

"Thanks Digger. I appreciate everyone's concern, really. But I'm fine and just needed to clear my head."

Bones finagled his way between Dad and Dixie. "I want to help too. I always get stuck in the kitchen and miss out on the real action."

I looked at my nineteen-year-old jack-of-all-trades. "Who's watching the grill. Are you burning something?"

He smiled broadly. "Nope, took everything off before I came out here."

Dixie glanced over at the order window. "Chicken spit! You missed something because there's smoke coming out of the kitchen!"

Bones sprinted for the swinging door into the kitchen. "I forgot about the...!"

I laughed. "He's getting better. But he always forgets the cheese melting on sandwiches under the salamander."

Chapter Five

Ida lived in an old farmhouse not far from Main Street. She bought it with her father ten years ago. Then after a long fight with cancer, her father died a couple of years ago, leaving Ida alone. She took it hard, and even though it seemed impossible, she became more cynical afterward.

She received a large inheritance and some life insurance money after he passed. With this, she remodeled the house but kept her Dad's bedroom as it was. Most of the rooms were upgraded to support her computer hobby, which included fancy wall jacks throughout the house with surge protection and Ethernet plugs. She also installed some special antennas, or some sort of technology I know nothing about, to make sure the wireless network is strong throughout the place. In her office, she keeps multiple monitors, a couple bigger than my television, and all kinds of black boxes with blinking lights that sit in banks of shelving. In one corner is a large device, which Ida told me was a battery backup, and was in addition to the generator installed out back. She made certain that electrical power would always be available to feed all her little toys. This was the real hack shack.

I took a seat. "Well, it's only been a couple of hours, but I couldn't wait. We thought we would come over to see if you got lucky before it gets too late tonight."

Ida typed. "A couple of hours sometimes pays off."

Piper held her stomach. "What kind of blue cheese did you use on that burger. My stomach is doing flips."

Ida shrugged. "My stomach is fine. I thought the burger was good."

Piper let out a loud burp. "Ahhh, that's better." For you maybe Piper.

I pointed to a large volume of text on the screens. "Well? Did you find anything in all this?"

Ida clicked her mouse. "Look at this. I searched the past couple of years of Jacob's life for keywords like will, bank, money, and insurance. And I already got some interesting hits under insurance. Seems in the last year, there were three insurance policies taken out by Jacob."

Piper asked, "Is that normal? Three in a year seems like a lot for a normal person."

Ida nodded. "I thought the same thing. When I sent out some web crawlers to learn about him, I found three policies. But it didn't make sense. There were requests for Jacob to sign two of the insurance policies, but I couldn't find payments made by him or a copy of those two particular policies. It's very odd."

I gasped. "Did you break into his bank files?"

Ida chuckled. "No. That's too dangerous even for me.

But Jacob set up notifications from his bank. Every time there was a transaction on his bank account, he was alerted. I hacked the messages the bank sent to him. They are less secure and easier to get into."

Piper focused. "So, what are you saying? He signed three policies, but only paid for one."

"That's a little oversimplified. But about right." Ida then clicked on file. "See this one? It's the one he took out on himself and named his girlfriend as the beneficiary. Oh, I guess I should mention he is living with his girlfriend of two years. Her name is Nicole Carr."

I laughed. "That makes sense. Last time I saw Jacob prior to this recent visit was a couple of years ago."

Piper glanced over at me. "So he moved on from you. But why take a life insurance policy out and name your live-in girlfriend?"

Ida clicked again. "See these texts? They made an agreement to insure each other. Nicole got a life insurance policy as part of her employment package. Seems she has no family and named him the beneficiary. But she asked he return the favor. Jacob didn't have a life insurance policy at work, so he simply bought one."

I wrinkled my nose. "That sounds like a little overkill for two people just living together."

Ida spun. "It did. So I looked a little more and it turns

out Nicole and Jacob have been an on again off again item for years. But this time they committed to a more serious relationship. He was not keen on getting married and she understood. But she wanted some form of commitment and the insurance policies was one of the things she came up with."

I snorted. "Please don't tell me that this was one of the girlfriends he cheated on me with."

Ida shrugged. "Okay. I won't tell you. It'll just make you mad."

"Son of a ditch digger. That insect. And I was starting to feel so bad for him lying in that hospital bed."

Piper chuckled. "Some wounds will never heal. But it's of no use getting worked up about it. You knew he cheated and you divorced him."

I pouted. "It doesn't ever stop hurting. I'm sorry. So, Ida, go on."

"Well, I had a bunch of questions about these other two policies he signed so I kept digging. The only thing I found was that his boss asked him to sign the policies. So it looks like they had something to do with work. That's all I know for now about those two life insurance policies. But there were a few other things."

I tried to moderate my voice to hide the anger still churning inside me. "Like what?"

"With work going well, he was making good money.

But it seems that some of the deals may be a little shady. Nicole sent him emails sometimes telling him to be careful. Especially about this one 'big' deal. They talked about it a few months ago. Jacob told her it could make them a lot of money, make their lives better, but he said that he couldn't say much about it per the client's request. It's odd and I am looking into it."

Piper clicked into journalist mode. "Wait a minute, that sounds exactly like the kind of thing we were looking for. If there was money involved in this 'big' deal, it might be something worth killing over."

Ida nodded. "Exactly, so it's why I am searching for more about it."

I fidgeted. "When do you think you'll find something."

"Hard to say for sure. But give me until tomorrow morning."

I sighed. "So the last two hours *were* productive for you. Thanks for the good work. And this all seems to be saying a trip to Savannah is definitely in the works. There's something going on there that came to Potter's Mill with Jacob's recent return."

Piper took out her phone and clicked a few times. "I can't go tomorrow, but the next day is fine. Can you leave the pub for a whole day, the day after tomorrow?"

"Sure. I will..." My phone cut me off. I took it out of my pocket and answered. "Hello?"

Aunt Mae spoke. "Ginger, so glad I caught you. Look something has come up. A detective from the Financial Crimes Unit of the Savannah-Chatham Police Department found something. It's an insurance policy that Jacob took out. It names you as a beneficiary. The detective is here and wants to speak with you. Can you come in for a few minutes?"

"It's getting kind of late. Can we do this tomorrow?"

"It's only 7:30. You can give us a few minutes and still make your bedtime, sweetie. The detective wants to go back to Savannah tonight after he speaks with you."

"Okay. I'll be there in about twenty."

"Thanks, honey. See ya in a few."

I clicked off. "Guess one of the odd policies you found names me as a beneficiary. That was Aunt Mae. She asked me to go meet with a detective from Savannah to talk about it with him."

Ida spun in her fancy desk chair. "How is that possible?"

"I have no idea. I don't know what they found but it must be a mistake. I'll let you know after I speak to the detective."

So I said goodbye to Piper and Ida and headed over to the police station. I had some time to think as I made the walk. Why would there be a life insurance policy where I was named the beneficiary? When I was married to

Jacob, neither of us had life insurance policies. So why now?

I arrived at the Potter's Mill police station and the lights were on inside. It was after hours and the front door was locked, but Aunt Mae was waiting for me and saw my approach through the glass entry. She flipped the deadbolt to let me in. "Hello. I appreciate you coming so late."

I entered. "Thanks for calling. Seems some interesting things are happening tonight. I hope you get the overtime rate for the extra hours."

Mae griped. "Since when has our little station paid overtime? Did I miss the memo?" We both laughed. Then Aunt Mae's face went long. "Sweetie, this is serious. I saw the policy and it was drafted and signed by Jacob only a few months ago. Then he shows up in town to talk to you, and bam! He's in the hospital. The detective is thinking those pieces all fit together. He sees you as a strong suspect. I told him we didn't think so, but he insisted on talking to you."

I again saw the man in plain clothes. It seemed liked a year ago, but it was only this morning when when I first saw him in the conference room. He came up behind my aunt. "Ginger, thanks for coming so late. We weren't properly introduce this morning. I'm Detective John Eckart from the Savannah Financial Crimes division. Deputy Owens here told me you would be happy to cooperate. I hope so because the events of the day are telling me I should be taking a long, hard look at you.

But your aunt here strongly disagrees, as does the Sheriff. I think they are being honest, but well you know, this is a small town. I grew up in a small town and I know everyone looks out for one another. So, a little distrust of what they're telling me seems prudent."

I shrugged. "I would have a little skepticism too if I was in your shoes. I understand."

Aunt Mae relocked the front door. "I think we would be more comfortable back in the conference room." She then led the way.

We all took seats and the detective started and slid a document across the table. "So, tell me about this insurance policy. Why did Jacob have one and name you, his ex-wife, the beneficiary?"

"I didn't know this insurance policy existed until Aunt Mae called me a few minutes ago." I picked it up and scanned the text.

"You mean to tell me this policy was drawn without your knowledge."

"I don't mean to tell you. I'm telling you point blank. I know nothing about it. But I'm really curious about it just like you, after learning it exists." I went to the end and looked at Jacob's signature.

The detective grimaced. "I find that hard to believe." He glared at me for a minute, looking for something, but I don't think he found it. "There is another thing I wanted to talk to you about. I hear stories about how talented you are in solving mysteries. How you have helped the local police in the past. Well, that's all great, and all, but now you say you're curious about this mysterious insurance policy that pays you in the event of Jacob's death. So let me be crystal clear, if you interfere with my investigation I will arrest you for obstruction of justice. Do you understand?"

I had a great rebuttal in my head, but all the came out was, "Yes."

He scowled. "Great. Now tell me again what you discussed with Jacob when you met with him."

And I told him again, and again. We reviewed my meeting with Jacob at the pub, the highlights of our marriage and divorce, my finances, and the weird insurance policy. It took longer than I expected.

Finally it was ten-thirty and we were all tired. The detective exhaled. "Alright, I think I'm good for now. I need to drive back to Savannah tonight, so I think we're done. But you need to stay put and let me know if you are going to leave town. For *any* reason. Got it?"

"Detective, I was going to visit Savannah in a couple of days. Is there any reason I can't make a day trip."

"No. That's fine, on one condition. You need to stop by the station and meet with me again. It will give me time to organize this mess and come up with more questions I want to ask you."

"I can do that."

The sullen man nodded. "Deal then. I'm in the office mid-afternoon that day. Meet me at two-thirty at the station."

I nodded. "Thanks. See you in two days, then."

I rose and left. Aunt Mae followed and grabbed me at the front door. "Ginger, sweetie. Be careful. This man thinks you may have done this. Don't do anything to convince him further."

I smiled. "I have no intention of dealing with Mr. Sunshine anymore than I have to. But I won't sit back and ignore false allegations."

The voice from the hallway cut like an envelope flap on a licking tongue. "I heard that. And I'll have you know that I have been called worse names. You couldn't do better." The detective came over and stood next to Mae. "Don't forget. Two-thirty. Two days from now. My office."

"I'll be there." I turned, unlocked the door, and stepped out into the cool night air. I needed some distance from the gruff detective. His insistence on making me a suspect was beyond troubling, it was unacceptable. There was new, urgent work to do tomorrow.

Chapter Six

Tossing and turning all night, I pondered why Jacob bought an insurance policy just a few months ago with me as the beneficiary. The more I thought about it the stranger it seemed; it made no sense. I woke early, eager to start digging into this new mystery.

I got out of bed, hastily ran through my morning routine, and left the apartment to immediately dive into the new development. It was seven-thirty in the morning and I loudly knocked on the door. Ida answered, wearing a blue robe and a blue scrunchie held her shoulder length brown hair in a pony tail. "Are you serious? I just got up."

I pushed my way in. "I need to talk with you and there's no time to waste."

Ida moaned. "I'm starting to regret offering my own office as the hack shack."

"Look, one of those insurance policies names me as the beneficiary. I saw it last night at the police station with my own eyes. Why?"

Ida rubbed her eyes. "Really? I haven't even had my coffee yet. But if you must, after you told me about your

Aunt's call last night, I set up some special searches to look for more info."

"Did you find anything?"

Ida chuckled. "Not if I haven't had my coffee. Coffee first."

So we went to her kitchen and made coffee together. I told Ida all about the meeting last night with the crusty detective, John Eckart. "He really thinks I may have done it for the insurance money."

Ida sipped her fresh coffee. "Son of a … I do it every morning. That damn thing brews so hot." She grimaced and pressed her hand to her mouth. "And this detective thing really sucks for you. But I was thinking, maybe Jacob felt guilty about cheating on you and did it as a kind of peace offering?"

"Do you realize how stupid that sounds? This is Jacob Allen we're talking about. While we were married he never even mentioned life insurance. And you already learned that his current girlfriend had to cut a deal with him to get him to take out a policy. He would never take one out on his own, especially benefiting his ex-wife."

"I guess you're right." She blew on her coffee then took a sip. "Let's go see what my friendly internet spider-men found."

We moved to the office and Ida sat and plunked a few keys. "Looks like we did find who issued the policies and they all came from one agency in Savannah, C.

Brown and Associates."

"Well, that's something we can check tomorrow when we visit Savannah."

Ida worked a bit more. "This is so odd. I still don't have a copy of the policy. But it looks like a man named Jake Belanger was involved too. His name appears in some of the correspondence I see."

"Okay, that's good. We need to find out who he is." My phone rang. I took it out and flipped it open to see it was Aunt Mae once again calling. "Hello, Auntie. You're calling early."

"I know, honey. But it's eight o'clock and I knew you would be up and about."

"So what's up?"

"I thought you might want to come by for a minute when you can. I got the report on Jacob's car from the state labs. And it's unusual, to say the least. Since you knew Jacob well, I thought you might like to take a look. See if what they found means anything to you."

"Okay, I'll be right over." I closed the flip phone and tilted my head back.

It must have been longer than I thought because I realized Ida was waiting breathlessly. She flipped her hands in the air, palms up. "Well?"

"I'm sorry. Was just thinking. Aunt Mae has the lab

report on Jacob's car. She asked me to head over and take a look."

"Well, I have plenty to do here so you should go see what you can learn from her."

"You're right. See ya later." And with that, I headed out once more for the police station. This was becoming an unwanted daily routine.

As was usual during business hours, Eunice greeted me at the station front desk and waved me on into the station. I found Aunt Mae hard at work and she looked surprisingly rumpled. She studied something on her computer screen while I took the seat on the side of her desk. She rubbed her red eyes. "Hello, sweetie. While we were meeting with Detective Eckart last night, the state techs emailed us the report on Jacob's car. I've been studying it since I got here early this morning. It makes no sense."

"Why?"

She popped up a picture of it on her screen and spun the monitor so I could see. "Take a look." After a moment, Aunt Mae spun the monitor back into place. "The device wired into Jacob's car is actually a collection of parts. They were set up to shock him through the steering column, like we suspected. But the electronic parts are a mix of modern and clever to low tech and clumsy."

"Well, electrocuting someone with their own car is pretty unusual. Not the kind of doohickey you buy off the shelf. So I guess you would have to use whatever you could find to make something like that work."

Aunt Mae sighed. "Yeah, but I was thinking this might be like bomb-making. People who build things like this to kill almost always have a signature in the way they construct their devices. But this sounds like it was just thrown together."

"Well, that explains why it didn't kill him. But it still worked well enough to put him in a coma."

"Yeah, unfortunate for your ex-husband. Shoot!" Aunt Mae scrolled down a little. "Whoever did this was smart enough to avoid leaving prints. The techs even looked for hairs or something with DNA left behind when the device was installed. But nothing."

There was brief pause till I sat up straight. "Hey, where is the car?"

"It's impounded at Donnie Freeman's garage."

"I was hoping to take a look."

"That's really not a good idea and you already saw the picture. It's evidence." She paused. "But we can go over and look if we don't touch. And we found tire prints in the mud next to where Jacob was parked. We can also visit the public parking lot to show you where."

"That sounds like a plan." I rose.

Aunt Mae moved some papers on her desk till she

found her car keys. "Let's go. I'll drive, it'll be faster."

I was surprised. Aunt Mae took the lone police car owned by Potter's Mill. I buckled in and felt out of place in the cruiser. I even slouched a little in my seat to try and stay out of sight. We arrived at Donnie Freeman's garage, which was also used by our police as an impound. Aunt Mae went into the office and emerged with another set of keys. She jumped back into the driver's seat. "Donnie keeps impounded cars locked up next door. I'm going to move the cruiser to block the entrance while we look at the car. I don't want the chain of custody for this evidence ruined by a curious visitor. You can meet me at the gate."

I exited the car and walked over to the impound area. Through the chain link fence, I could see there were only a few cars inside. And it was obvious that most of the cars inside had been there for a while.

Aunt Mae moved the police car, blocking the driveway, and then got out and came over to unlock the gate. She flung it open and we stepped inside. She pointed her finger at the cars. "Now, don't touch anything. It would contaminate the evidence. Understand."

"Yes. I got it. No touching." I eyed the odd sight. There were a number of large piles covered with plastic sheeting.

Aunt Mae took the plastic off one pile, revealing the seats from Jacob's car sitting on yet another piece of plastic underneath. She laughed. "It looks like the techs were thorough."

"Holy cow! They took his car apart!"

Aunt Mae cocked her head to one side. "Only way to look and not miss anything."

I saw a large, locked metal box, like the kind they use at construction sites. "What's that?"

"That's where they locked up the device. Let's take a look. I have the key for that too." Aunt Mae put the key in the old-fashioned padlock and twisted, freeing the metal bolt. She opened the lid and we peeked inside. "There it is, sweetie. I wanted to see it in person too and it looks different from the picture in the report."

"Aunt Mae, I'm not sure what I'm looking at, but it doesn't look like much."

"Well, Jacob can be glad for that or he would have ended up dead."

"A bunch of the parts are copper."

"Yeah, but copper conducts electricity well. Makes sense to use in a device like this. Okay, I think we are done here." Aunt Mae closed and re-locked the lid. "I have to go back inside to return the keys and fill out some paperwork to document our visit."

I pointed to another odd looking pile. "What's that?"

Aunt Mae pulled off the covering and we saw sales binders and folders. I recognized the name printed on the binders. It was the distributor who now supplied my beer and liquor, Bev Serve. "That's to be expected for a salesman. Now we should go, sweetie." Aunt Mae recovered the sales binders and car seats with plastic and we headed out of the impound pen.

I got back into the cruiser while Aunt Mae returned the keys to the office. Then she returned to the car, buckled in and we were off. While turning onto Main Street she glanced over at me. "Ginger, did any of that mean anything to you?"

"Well, Jacob was definitely a good salesman and his car is packed with sales literature. So he was working a respectable job. Nothing funny about any of that. The device, though, I don't know. I still think it's odd to see so much copper."

"I appreciate your input." She turned off Main Street. "We're here."

Our next destination was the public parking lot. It sat between the Potter's Mill Oracle and the custom motorcycle shop owned by Guardrail and Dog Breath. The lot sits a couple of doors down from The Fluffy Pillow, but the B&B uses the large lot to provide enough parking for all its guests.

Aunt Mae drove through the lot and I saw an area taped off in neon yellow. "Well, there's no doubt where he parked. You police like that tape."

Aunt Mae chuckled. "I know, it's cliche but the yellow tape works. Keeps people out of an area even though it's just a flimsy piece of plastic."

We parked and exited the car. I walked over to the roped off area. "Well, not much to see but lots of pavement."

Aunt Mae smiled. "So you think. Yes, it's an asphalt lot, but see that spot over there." She pointed. "It's a low spot. Water puddles there and a thin layer of dirt has collected over time. There's enough dirt there now to form mud when wet, and there was a tire print in that mud thanks to the morning dew, right next to Jacob's car."

I huffed. "Well, that's kind of interesting. I guess. But how can we know if it was the one who rigged his car?"

"We can't. But that mud puddle is pretty fragile and it's a fair assumption that the tire print is pretty fresh or it wouldn't have been good enough for us to get an impression to analyze."

I folded my arms. "That makes sense. Did the print mean anything?"

"Well, the computer says it's most likely from a truck. That particular tire is used almost exclusively on full-size pickups. And there was an irregular spot, most likely a plug to fix a hole in the tread."

"In rural Georgia, that doesn't narrow it down too much, does it?"

Aunt Mae laughed. "The Sheriff said exactly the same

thing."

I swiveled my head for one last look. "Well, I guess we're done here. Thanks. It's just as easy for me to walk back to the pub from here. I'll see ya later. There's a lot to think about."

Aunt Mae nodded. "You got that right. *Lots* to mull on. If you think of anything, or realize something new after seeing all this, let me know. Thanks, sweetie."

"Will do. Hey, by the way, tomorrow Piper and I are heading to Savannah. Is there anything you want me to do? Or do you need anything from there?"

"No, honey, but it's sweet of you to offer. Eckart is taking care of things on that end. And by the way, make sure you're on time to see him tomorrow."

"Thanks for the reminder. But I'm keenly aware of our meeting. And I don't want to do anything to make Mr. Sunshine more grouchy."

"Okay, honey. I'm heading back to the station. Be careful tomorrow. Some of the information I am getting out of Savannah is concerning. That device found on Jacob's car indicates that some real hardcore criminals might be involved. Please watch yourself."

"I always do Auntie. And Piper will be with me. We'll be fine."

Aunt Mae kissed my cheek and then got back in her car. She waved at me as she left the lot.

Chapter Seven

I changed my mind. Instead of heading back to the pub, I made my way back to Ida's house. I knocked and she yelled through the door. "It's open." I let myself in and could see that she showered and dressed while I was gone.

I joined her in the kitchen where she was playing with her phone and getting more coffee. "You smell good."

Ida flicked her hair. "It's the shampoo. Scooter likes it."

"Geez, he's even picking your soap now?"

"No, I like it too, and if makes him happy, well..."

I rolled my eyes. "Back in the sane world, I was wondering. Can you search the internet for things based on a description?"

"Maybe, depends on what you mean by description."

"I saw the device installed on Jacob's car. It's unusual and Aunt Mae said things like that are usually a signature. I was wondering if you could find something online based on how it was used, along with the basic description of it."

"Yeah, that should be possible."

Ida and I headed for her office, now our current hack shack. Ida typed in the description of what I saw and how the device was employed. She gasped. "That's not good."

"What did you find?"

"A story from a local television station in Savannah about a moonshiner who was killed when he started his truck. He was electrocuted. And the device looked like this." She pointed at her screen. I saw a picture of the device found by police in that case.

I stared at the image. "I can feel the hairs on the back of my neck standing up."

Ida leaned back. "So I'm guessing it looks similar to what you saw with Mae."

"Yeah. Not exact but pretty close. And lots of copper, just like I saw this morning."

"So what does this tell us?"

"Well, it depends. Did they find who committed this crime?"

Ida read for a few seconds. "Nope, but the article says they suspected another shiner, named Sammy Mason. But he goes by Rotgut."

"Rotgut? That's a horrible nickname, yuck."

Ida chuckled. "If he's the one who did this, then he's named appropriately."

"I guess. After all, you wouldn't call a homicidal moonshiner something like Snuggle Buns."

"Nope. Rotgut seems more appropriate." Ida read on. "Oh, look at this. This is not his only suspected crime. It says here that Rotgut is suspected of killing two other people. Ouch, and one was with a shotgun. Seems they haven't found enough to charge him though."

"This must have been what Aunt Mae meant."

Ida spun and looked at me like I was an orange in a barrel of apples. "What?"

"She told me to be careful. That some really bad people were involved in this. Rotgut seems to qualify as real bad people."

Ida made a face. "I suspect bad people is the nicest thing Rotgut ever gets called."

I sighed. "You're probably right."

There was a knock at the door. Ida looked up. "I sent a text to Piper, told her you were here. That must be her." Ida got up out of her plush office chair and went to answer the door.

I looked at the picture of Rotgut in the article. It was a fuzzy picture, but his size, the bald head, and evil stare made it clear that he was not the kind of person who worries about his Facebook page.

Piper came into the office chuckling. "There's really a man who goes by the name, Rotgut?"

I nodded. "Yep. And I wouldn't laugh at him. It looks like he may have killed three people. That's his pic." I pointed to the monitor.

Piper grimaced. "Wow! That man must take ugly pills. I wouldn't want to meet him anywhere, anytime. He looks like he eats kittens for lunch."

Ida sighed. "Well, he might be involved in this. And he's out of Savannah. So you two need to be careful tomorrow."

Piper took a seat. "You know, I'm wondering, Ida. Maybe you should come with us tomorrow. I assume you can use a computer while we're on the road, right?"

"Sure. I'll just take a laptop and my phone. It's all I need."

"That might be of use. Depending on what we find. And if we are dealing with some hardcore criminals..." Piper looked at the screen again and shuddered. "And it looks like we are, we should go prepared for anything."

I looked at Ida. "So can you come with us tomorrow? I mean, you don't have to go shopping for some special shampoo do you?"

Ida shrugged. "I was thinking of going with you. But

keep making fun of my personal hygiene products and I might change my mind."

Piper leaned forward. "I'm not sure what shampoo has to do with anything, so I'm going to ignore that part for now. More important, what's our plan of attack when we get to Savannah?"

I let out a deep breath. "Well, we should go see where Jacob lives and talk to his current girlfriend, Nicole. If we can."

Piper and Ida both stared at me. Piper finally dared to ask, "Are you going to be alright?"

"What do you mean? I don't have any animosity for this girl. I don't even know her."

Piper laughed. "Well, the only time you ever made me nervous was that time in high school when I thought you were going to rip Vicky Sue a new one. Remember when she kissed Jacob to thank him?"

I huffed. "She was soooo out of line."

"No, she wasn't. Jacob helped her Dad get the harvest done before bad weather moved in. It saved the family's year. She just gave him a kiss on the cheek to thank him."

Ida giggled. "Oh snap! A jealous Ginger. I would've loved to seen that."

I turned red. "I was young and in love. I've matured

since then. Or I've tried to."

Piper snorted. "Where Jacob is involved, I don't know. He was your first love and your first marriage. You have to admit, he's your Kryptonite."

"Ginger as Super-girl? Not." Ida used her smug voice.

I tried my best to use a humble voice. "I guess you didn't like the jab about your new shampoo then?"

Ida folded her arms. "No, I did not!"

Piper continued. "What is it with you two today. You're missing my point, Ginger. We want to get information from Nicole. Not make her mad or insult her."

I shot back. "I'll be fine. What else do we need to do in Savannah?"

Ida responded. "Well, I would like to visit this C. Brown and Associates. The place that issued all the insurance policies."

I nodded. "That's good. Okay, we're going to be busy. And we need to visit Bev Serve. The place where Jacob works. So anything else?"

Ida cleared her throat. "Do you think we should try and talk to Rotgut too?"

I felt raw fear flash within me. "Are you kidding?"

Ida winched. "No. He might be in the center of this. If

we don't actually meet with him, then maybe we can at least learn who he is, where he works, who knows him, things like that."

Piper stiffened. "No, Ida is right. If we can talk to him, that would be good. We might learn something. There will be three of us, in broad daylight. And if we can meet him somewhere public, we should be fine."

I raised my eyebrows. "I would rather not, but if you think it will help."

Piper added, "So four stops. It will be a long day, but we should be able to do that in a day."

I responded. "No, five. I need to go the Savannah police station at two-thirty, meet with Detective Eckart."

Piper groaned, just a little. "I forgot about that. Well, that makes things harder. So it'll be very long day."

I said, "So we have a plan. What time do we leave?"

Piper mulled. "It takes forty-five to sixty minutes to get there. If we leave at eight, we can get most of our work in before having to go over to the police station."

I looked at Piper. "So, you and Ida have the good cars. Ida needs to work on the computer. That means you should drive. Should we meet at The Oracle at seven-thirty then?"

Piper hesitated. "Alright. I guess I can drive."

Ida tittered. "So it's girls day out in Savannah. This

ought to be interesting. Do you think we'll have time for some shopping? I need new clothes for an award show I'm going to with Scooter and Savannah has really nice stores."

I furrowed my brow. "Are you serious. We have lots to do and we're trying to find someone who attempted to murder another person."

Piper shrugged. "Well, Ida is right. No need to waste an opportunity. Maybe Ida and I can go shopping while you see your friend at the police station."

I uttered, "I can see we're intensely focused. This ought to go well when we interview the guy named Rotgut."

Ida waved at me. "Oh lighten up, it'll be fun. And we'll get to everything you need done, too."

Piper looked at her phone. "It's still only noon. Is there anything we should do with the rest of this day?"

I looked at Ida. "Can you help me make the phone calls and send emails to set up our meetings for tomorrow?"

"Yes, but the moonshiner might be hard to track down. The others should be straightforward."

"Good, that will help."

Piper tapped on her phone. "I need to get my oil changed so I'll call and see if Donnie can get the work done today. No reason to risk a break down during a trip to the coast."

Ida threw her hands over her head. "Woo-hoo, road trip!"

"Somehow I still don't think you understand we are chasing a potential murderer, Ida. And his name is Rotgut. You saw his picture. Remember?"

Ida giggled. "Doesn't matter why, it's still a road trip to Savannah. Love that town."

Chapter Eight

We hit the road early the next morning and were well on our way to the coast. I sat in the front passenger seat and Piper kept her eyes on the road as she spoke. "You were early to my office this morning. Eager to make this trip?"

"Not really. I'm not the traveling type. You know that. But I do want results. And at this point, Savannah may provide answers to some tough questions."

Piper snickered. "I think you're afraid of Sammy the Rotgut."

I scrunched up my face. "Is that how you say his name? I didn't even think about how to address him. Is it Mr. Rotgut?"

Piper laughed harder. "After seeing his pic, I'll call him whatever makes him comfortable."

Ida was in the back seat typing on her laptop. "Just like I thought. That Rotgut guy is hard to find. Seems he keeps a low profile."

I glanced over my shoulder to watch her work. "I don't think murdering moonshiners hang a shingle and wait for people to find them."

Ida shot back. "Well, no, of course not. But the insurance office does and we're cutting it close. The man who runs the place is Christopher Brown. He said he could meet first thing at nine. So that's stop number one and we need to step on it to make it in time."

Piper pointed to a road sign. "Speed limit is fifty-five. I'm doing sixty. Going as fast we can and not get stopped. I'm not paying for a speeding ticket."

I adjusted my seat belt. "We're fine, should be there right on time. So what are we going to ask him?"

Ida answered. "Well, first confirm he issued all three policies."

I added. "Then I would like to know who paid for them. You still didn't find a payment from Jacob for two of them, right Ida?"

"Yep. But I'm not sure he'll volunteer that information. That might be, as they say, confidential."

Piper jumped in. "We'll see what we can do with Mr. Brown. Then what's next after him?"

Ida answered. "Nicole Carr, at the condo where she and Jacob are shacked up."

Piper looked in the rear-view mirror. "Ida, that's insensitive. We don't want Ginger riled up when we meet with her."

Ida chuckled. "I don't know, might be fun to see what happens."

I turned in my seat to scowl at her. "That's not going

to happen. I just want to find out who might have wanted to harm Jacob and frame me for it."

Ida raised her eyebrows. "Ah, so there it is. You don't like being a suspect. I guess I get that. I wouldn't like it either, so sorry."

"I accept your apology. If you pay for dinner." I eyed her playfully.

Ida pinched her eyebrows together for a second. "I guess I can live with that. Deal." She laughed and Piper joined her.

Piper started singing with the radio and Ida and I fell silent to watch some road signs whiz by. Then we briefly discussed the meetings for the rest of the day, but for some reason, we moved on and discussed what was on the radio and how much money Ida would spend on dinner. And before we knew it, we pulled into the parking lot of a small white building with a sign out front that read C. Brown and Associates.

Piper plunked her left hand on the steering wheel and turned so that she could see both the front and back seat. "We're here, with two minutes to spare. Showtime!"

I took a deep breath. "Let's do this. Ida, you should wait here. Three of us might be a little too much. And see if you can track down someone we can talk to, or anyone that knows Mr. Rotgut."

"Fine, leave me out of the fun. Alright. I can also find the best stores to shop at while you're in there."

Piper and I exited the car and went inside. We found a small office with a young woman working at a spot just inside the door and an older, disheveled man working at another station in the rear of the open space. I raised my voice and addressed both of them. "We have a meeting with a Christopher Brown at nine o'clock."

The frumpy man rose. "I'm Mr. Brown. But I prefer to be called Chris by pretty ladies."

"My name is Ginger and this is Piper. We appreciate you taking the time to meet with us."

"My pleasure, please have a seat." He grabbed two seats lined up against the wall and moved them to the front of his desk. We followed his lead and sat. He continued. "So what can I do for you?"

Piper clicked into journalist mode. "So, in the last year we understand you issued three life insurance policies that cover Jacob Allen, a salesman from Bev Serve. Can you confirm this for us?"

Chris eyed us for a moment. "Who are you again?"

I leaned forward a bit. "I'm Ginger O'Mallory. Jacob's ex-wife and a named beneficiary on one of the policies."

"Ah, I'm sorry for your loss. So you're here looking to get paid?"

I snorted. "No, that's not it at all. Jacob was hurt and it looks like someone was trying to kill him. But it didn't work. So I'm not sure why I would be getting paid."

Chris pulled a long face and shuffled in his seat. After letting out a deep breath, he said, "Oh, I just assumed. So many policies to manage, and so many people filing claims. I can't keep them all straight. And people are always looking to get paid."

Piper pressed. "So did you issue the policies?"

He leaned back in his chair. "I can't reveal any client information."

I asked, "Well, if I am named as the beneficiary of a policy, do I have a right to see that policy?"

He interlocked his fingers and rested his hands on his big belly. "I guess, maybe, um, I don't really know. It was not purchased by you. So it's kind of complicated. I think that's a question for a lawyer."

Piper pounced. "So, you're saying you did issue the policy."

"I...I...I'm not saying I did or didn't. I'm just saying this sounds complicated and you should ask someone who knows the laws better than me."

"But you're an insurance agent. You don't know?"

"No. I think you should leave now."

I looked over at Piper. "I think we can go now. We're not looking to cause trouble."

She nodded back. "Yeah, you're right." Piper then sneered at Chris. "I don't like the smell in this place."

Chris scowled at us as we got up and left. We wasted no time getting back to the car where we found Ida with ear buds in doing a butt dance in the back seat. I raised my voice. "Hey, you find anything while we were in there?"

Ida jumped and pulled the white plugs from her ears. "You scared me! What?"

"You find anything?"

"Yeah. I love Imagine Dragons. That song Thunder gets me moving."

Piper flashed at her. "We're in there dealing with a slime ball and you're out here doing a disco butt jig?"

"Technically, Imagine Dragons is *not* disco."

"You know what I mean."

I cut in. "Alright, let's focus. Ida, did you find anything?"

"Nope. Rotgut is a ghost."

I grunted. "That's not helpful. Alright, what's next?"

Ida muttered only one word. "Nicole." After she put away her ear buds and reshuffled a few things in the back seat, she asked, "How about you two? Did you learn anything?"

Piper answered, "Yeah, this guy is a guilty scum bag. He assumed Jacob was dead. Why? And he didn't admit to it, but he issued the policies. I'm sure of it."

I added, "I got the same impression. Mr. Brown in there expected me to say Jacob was dead when I told him I was the ex-wife named on the policy. Why? The only answer I come up with is he thought Jacob would be dead by now. So he knew an attempt on Jacob's life was going to made, but didn't hear how it turned out."

"I agree. So not what we expected, but we did learn lots. This Brown guy is scum and is involved up to his eyeballs. Now let's go see what we can learn from this Nicole Carr." Piper started the car and put it in gear.

We were at the townhouse where Jacob lived with Nicole quick enough. We pulled up to the guard shack, I was surprised to find a gated community, but we checked in and drove through the extravagantly landscaped entrance. We found the unit and parked, then decided that it would be alright if all three of us went in this time. We made our way past the manicured flower beds to the entrance and I knocked on the raised panel door.

A voice came through the door. "I'll be right there!"

I looked back to Ida and Piper. "She knows we're coming, right?" Ida nodded yes. I turned back to the door and waited.

I heard the deadbolt flip and the door opened to reveal a short, but fit, blonde haired woman with sparkling blue eyes. She wore Lululemon running pants and a sports bra that left nothing to the imagination. I stammered for a second and finally said, "Hello, I'm Ginger, Jacob's ex-wife."

"Right on time. Glad you made it. I so wanted to meet you. Jacob has mentioned you more than a few times."

"I'm glad to meet you, too?" I was fumbling for the right tone.

Piper came to the rescue. "We're so sorry about Jacob. We're all hoping for a quick, full recovery."

Nicole smiled. "Thank you. I was going to run up to the hospital later to see him tonight. The doctors are not telling me much right now."

Ida blurted out, "Wow, nice place. This must cost a few pennies each month."

Piper jabbed Ida with her elbow. "Where are your manners?"

Ida chuckled. "Who said I had any?"

Nicole chuckled too. "It looks like you've spent some long hours in the car this morning. Would you like some ice tea?"

I nodded yes. "Sounds great."

Nicole stepped back, held the door open wide, and held her hand out. "Well, come on in and have a seat. Relax a bit."

We sat on the plush sofa and Nicole went into the kitchen. I scanned the nicely furnished living room and noted that Jacob did not pick any of the items; he did not have good taste and this place was screaming fine living. She returned a couple of minutes later with a silver tray. It was a full platter with a pitcher of ice tea, ice cubes, glasses, a squeeze bottle, and cut lemons. She beamed, "I have unsweetened tea here, but there is simple syrup in the squeeze bottle and cut lemons, so you can fix it up the way you like. And there's more ice for those who like lots of ice."

Piper looked over at me, wide-eyed. "Look at this, The Grumpy Chicken should serve ice tea like this. It's fancy."

Nicole cocked her head to one side. "What's The Grumpy Chicken?"

I snuffled. "It's the pub I own and run with my father. I'm surprised Jacob didn't mention it."

"Jacob mentions so many pubs and bars. But to be honest, I never really listened to all that. I'm not into the bar scene and found his work a bit boring. But The Grumpy Chicken is such an unusual name."

Piper picked up on it. "I see. So you didn't know much about his work?"

"No. Not really."

"Can you tell me about the insurance policies he took out?"

Nicole wrinkled her nose. "You said policies, with an 'S.' I'm aware of only one life insurance policy, the one he took out to cover me in the event of his death. See, we financed this place together, so we had to insure ourselves. I can't afford it on my own if I lost him."

Piper continued. "I see. So what do you do for a living?"

"I'm an aerobics instructor."

Ida bleated. "We should have guessed by the outfit." This time I jabbed her with an elbow.

Nicole blushed. "Oh, I was just out for a run. I like to run before I go to work. I have a class to do this afternoon."

I scooted to the edge of my seat. "Nicole, it looks like Jacob had three life insurance policies. Do you know *anything* about the other two?"

"No. Just the one he took out when I asked him to. You know just before we bought this place."

I rose and went to shake her hand. "Thank you very much for talking to us. I know this is hard. Please let us know if we can do *anything* to help. I hate that this happened and will do whatever I can. But for now, we'll be on our way and let you get to work, and to the hospital later. We have to keep moving, too, as there's lots to get done while we're here in Savannah."

Piper and Ida looked at each other like they were

about to call a penalty for a tea party foul, but they eventually stood too and said goodbye.

I added, "Seriously, we want to help so don't be afraid to ask for anything. We're not that far away and want to make it easier for you to get through this, if we can."

Nicole smiled. "Thanks so much for that. Jacob has some good friends, it seems, that he kept hidden from me. It was really nice to meet you and I hope to see you again, soon."

I smiled back. "Somehow, I have a feeling we will cross paths again. I look forward to it. See ya around." I gave a slight wave and opened the front door to leave. Piper and Ida did not speak but the looks they gave me as we walked to the car spoke volumes. They would have liked to stay a little longer, but we really did need to go.

Chapter Nine

We buckled in once again and I looked back to Ida in the rear seat. "So what time is Bev Serve expecting us?"

"Twelve-thirty. Leaves us plenty of time before we have to drop you off at the police station."

Piper huffed. "So I'm the one who has to bring it up? Why did you cut the meeting with Nicole off?"

"You know. She's *perhaps* an interesting person, maybe. But she's no murderer."

Ida cut in. "Yeah, her interesting personality was clearly showing in that tight outfit. I wish I could afford Lululemon."

I chose to ignore Ida and continued. "It's clear Nicole loves her life and needs Jacob to afford it. She has no motive to kill him but does have a strong motive to keep him alive and kicking. And for some reason, I had assumed she was more insurance savvy when Ida found that she asked for a reciprocating policy from Jacob. But on their salaries, it's obvious that a bank financed this place and the loan probably required life insurance policies on both of them since they weren't married. To secure the debt."

Piper slumped in her seat. "Yeah. I know. I thought exactly the same thing. But I was enjoying my tea. That place was nice.'"

Ida chimed in. "Ginger, you should have seen your face when that blonde bombshell answered the door."

I said the first thing that came to mind. "Her hair was bleached. I bet you saw the dark roots just like I did."

Ida laughed. "Of course I noticed."

I asked Ida, "So, who's meeting with us at the distributors?"

"The Bev Serve email said someone from human resources. I had to call them a few times. They weren't real happy about it but did finally send me an email to pick a time on Calendly."

I crinkled my nose. "What's a Calendly?"

"A website to schedule meetings where you can just pick a time out of the open slots available. It makes it easy and prevents sending a bunch of emails back and forth."

I rocked my head. "So that's why I didn't know. It's a digital thing. I am so out of it when it comes to anything with a keyboard or mouse. I need to work on my computer skills."

Piper had already started the car and set up the GPS on her phone. We were on the way over to Bev Serve when she broke a moment of silence. "Can I be honest?"

I nodded. "I would expect nothing less from the best

journalist in Potter's Mill."

"I expected the insurance agency to be greedy enough to sell the three insurance policies, but otherwise innocent. And I expected Nicole to be an important meeting, the real person of interest. But that didn't happen and it's actually the opposite. Nicole is innocent and this Brown guy is just screaming guilty."

I chuckled. "I know. But one thing doesn't make sense to me. Why would Brown do it? He stands to gain nothing. He already sold the polices and that's the only money he makes in this. He wreaks but there is no strong motive."

Ida's voice drifted from the back seat. "I hate when you talk like the police. 'Motive.' You like to use that word. Why can't you just say he had no reason to do it like a normal person."

"Because this is serious and deserves to be treated appropriately. Life has taught me to resolve riddles and loose ends and do it professionally if you can. If you leave them hanging, they end up haunting you like the grumpy chicken. So I try to treat things with the seriousness they deserve and act professionally."

Ida laughed out loud. "Okay Ms. Grouchy. Was just saying."

Piper cut in. "I hate to bring this up. But that sounds like you were saying you hate never learning what your mom tried to tell you before she died. I remember how much it gnawed at you. We get it and that's why we're here for you. To help."

I looked at the dashboard, avoiding eye contact. "I know. And thank you." I paused. "Mom's death in the middle of my divorce did change me. And I know I can be a tad persistent when I want answers."

Ida roared. "Persistent? More like obsessed, or stubborn."

Piper cut her off. "Ida! We're trying to help, remember?"

Ida reached over the front seat to put her hand on my shoulder, still chuckling. "I'm sorry. I really am. Piper's right. And remember, I'm paying for lunch."

"I'm so lucky to have such good friends." My voice may have had a hint of sarcasm when I looked back at Ida.

Piper fawned. "Awww, that's so sweet, girls, but can we pause this lovely moment. We're here and need to put our investigator hats back on."

I looked out the windshield to realize Bev Serve was huge. The office was a massive two-story brick building with two large metal warehouses behind it. Trucks were whizzing to and from loading docks and the office parking lot was near full. One truck coming from the gated courtyard that surrounded the warehouse area practically ran us over as he sped out onto the main road.

We found a parking spot after some searching. All three of us got out and stretched our legs, then we entered and signed in, which included showing identification. A woman dressed in a professional looking pantsuit came out to greet us, after which she lead us to the human resource's office. We started the conversation slow and quickly realized this was going nowhere since her answer to every question was "that's confidential."

Piper pressed her. "Look, I understand personal information about an employee is confidential. But we came here all the way from Potter's Mill to try and find out why someone may have hurt Jacob. We just want to know if anything weird or unusual was going on with him. That's more than fair for an ex-wife like Ginger to ask."

The HR lady studied me. "Are you the one that was on that TV show, the one with the pub in Potter's Mill?"

"Yep, that was me. But that has nothing to do with why we're here. I was hoping to talk to Jacob's boss. Can you at least tell me who he or she is?"

The woman sighed. "I'm not supposed to tell you this. But you seem like nice people… and you being his ex. Plus I loved that episode so much." She paused. "You could find out easy enough, too, if you wanted to. So okay, that would be Mr. Belanger, the company president. Jacob reported directly to him."

I shot a look to Ida and Piper. Ida nodded in confirmation. I asked, "What is Mr. Belanger's first name?"

"Jake."

Ida gulped. "Well, what would it take to get a meeting with Mr. Belanger?"

"Mr. Belanger is a very busy man and he is out of town until next week. If you call his office, they might be able to set up a meeting."

Piper rose. "Thank you, we appreciate you taking the time for us."

Ida and I followed suit, shaking the woman's hand, and we left. As we were buckling back into our seats, Ida remarked. "Well, now we know who the Jake Belanger I found is. And this is not good. This place is a major business here in Savannah and this guy is probably connected three ways to Sunday."

Piper snorted. "I agree, that could be a problem. But we still need to find the truth here and my gut is telling me that something is definitely going on here. That HR representative was obviously told to say nothing and she made it clear it would be hard for us to get a meeting with this Belanger guy. It smells off."

"Well, this day is just full of surprises. And now I get to meet with Detective Eckart. I'm pretty sure he's related to Darth Vader, but the detective has less personality." I sighed and looked out the car window as we left the parking lot.

Piper chuckled. "Stop being so dramatic. It's not that bad. It'll be fine. He's just doing his job."

"Easy for you to say. You and Ida get to go shopping while I do a scene from The French Connection. And the detective thinks I'm the bad guy. That's better than shopping, right?"

Ida's spoke softly, almost below an audible level. "Well, if it makes you feel better, we can pick up something for you."

I spun to look at the rear seat. "That's nice of you, but it's not necessary."

Piper smacked my arm with the back of her hand. "Hey, what do you think about this. Maybe your detective friend knows Rotgut. Maybe he can tell you something about him."

I chortled. "Him helping me, now that would be something to see."

Piper pointed out the windshield. "Well, we're a tad early, but that's the station. So you're about to find out if he will or won't."

"I guess it's time for me to walk the green mile. Tell my father I went to the chair with my head held high."

Ida quipped. "Keep talking like that and I'll put ya in the electric chair myself. Geeze!"

Piper laughed. "Go. Do what you need to do. When

should we be back?"

"I assume this will take about an hour, so in sixty minutes?"

Ida moaned and Piper nodded. "Well, that doesn't give us much time for shopping, but we'll be here." To underline the point, Piper glared at Ida as she moved to the front seat.

I walked up to the front door reluctant to go in. I was early but decided that maybe the charming detective would understand and be accommodating. After talking to the sergeant manning the front desk, I was surprised to find I was right. Detective Eckart was on his way out to escort me to his office.

We walked quite a ways through a maze of desks and work stations, then I sat in a metal chair with uncomfortable green padding next to his desk. "Well, I'm not sure why, but I'm here like you asked."

Eckart opened a folder and took out a large black and white photograph. "See this man?" He handed the picture to me. "His name is Sammy Mason, but he goes by Rotgut. This man makes moonshine and runs numbers for a living. And we think he also kills people. This is the suspect for what happened to Jacob."

I shrugged. "I figured that out on my own just using the internet."

"Don't get smart with me, I'm trying to help you here. This man will stop at nothing to hurt someone like you if it's what he needs to do. And I think you poking around Savannah might lead him to believe he needs to do something about you. You don't want that and neither do I."

"I appreciate your concern. But it's surprising after our first meeting where I came away feeling like a prime suspect."

"Yes, you were a prime suspect two days ago. But now you're a person of interest. But Rotgut is my prime suspect."

"I get the distinction, thank you."

"Look, I've seen a lot in this line of work. And I let the facts speak for themselves. A pretty young woman like you looks all sweet and innocent when I first meet her, but I know that doesn't mean there isn't a bloodthirsty killer lurking inside."

"Ouch!"

"But I'm not stupid. I can see someone tried to frame you for this. In today's world, with cell phones, email, texts, social media...all that crap, we can see into a person's thoughts more than ever. And you, you were even on a TV show. So I've since learned a little about Ginger O'Mallory since we last met. When originally I asked for this meeting, I thought it was going to be a chance to grill you more on the insurance policy and your finances. But I was wrong."

"This day is just one surprise after another."

He tried to smile, but his stern face would not allow it. "So, where did you go today and what did you do?"

So I told Det. Eckart that we had three meetings and explained our failed attempts to find Rotgut. But I left most of the good tidbits of what we learned out. He took notes as I talked, then he put the pen down and eyed me. "You tried to *meet* with Rotgut?"

"Yeah."

"You're braver than half the cops in here!"

"I've faced murderers before."

"I know. The Potter's Mill police gushed about how you helped them on multiple occasions."

"It's a small town. We have to stick together and help one another. Even the police."

"I grew up in a small town not far from here, so I understand. But Savannah is a different ball of muck. You can't go poking around into things and not get into trouble. Or get dead."

"I understand. I was just trying to figure out why I'm named the beneficiary of an insurance policy I have no knowledge of taken out by ex-husband."

"Well, I can't stop you officially, but take my advice and don't do it."

"I appreciate the guidance."

"Here, can you take this back to Deputy Owens?" He threw a large manila envelope on the desk.

"Sure, what is it?"

"None of your business! She's expecting it from you. It will get there faster this way."

"Okay."

He played with his pen. "Thanks for the favor. So, did you learn anything else today that you should tell me?"

I paused, then just said it. "Maybe, Jake Belanger of Bev Serve looks like he may have had something to do with the three life insurance policies concerning Jacob. And the insurance agency, Chris Brown in particular, smells rotten. It was really interesting that this Brown guy assumed Jacob was already dead. It seemed like something is off with both of them."

He looked up at me, squinting. "You might have mentioned that part when you told me you met with them. But Maybe Sheriff Morrison was right. You have some talent for this investigation thing. So thanks for sharing, but I already know all that."

"Thanks, I think. Now I've told you everything, so are we done here?"

"Yeah. I appreciate you coming by. And if there is anything you think of, or find out, let me know ASAP. Here's my card." He flipped the card over and scribbled a phone number on it. "That's my personal cell phone.

Call me anytime if you have to."

"Thanks. Now I feel guilty." I tucked the business card into one of my bluejean's pockets.

"Why."

"Earlier I told friends I thought you were related to Darth Vader. But I was wrong. Sorry. You're just doing a tough job. I know that now."

For just a moment, he laughed. "You made my day. I love your honesty. And by the way, I became a cop because I have relatives that made Vader look like a Boy Scout. But I wanted to do some good for society after seeing how much harm they did to others. So I joined the force." He wasn't laughing now.

I blankly looked at him and tried to say something but just stuttered a bit. Finally, I said, "I'll let you know immediately if I learn anything. I promise."

"That's what I needed to hear. Now get out of here. This conversation is getting too mushy for my liking." He waved his hand towards the front of the building. "You know the way out. See ya around kid."

"Thanks. See ya."

I picked up the large envelope for Aunt Mae and walked out on my own, but I took my time. This was *not* the Potter's Mill police station. There were dozens of uniformed officers mixed with detectives and almost as many civilians. Phones rang, people gushed to proclaim their innocence, cops yelled at perps to keep quiet, and noises I could not quite identify all blended to create a painful din. I had no idea how anyone got work done here but I found new respect Det. Eckart for being so focused in this environment.

I was surprised when I realized the meeting lasted seventy minutes but that meant Piper's car should be waiting out front. But as with everything I did today, I was surprised. Piper and Ida were absent when I got to the parking lot.

Chapter Ten

I sat on the curb with the envelope in my lap and waited. I didn't know why my friends were late, but I had a pretty good idea. Ida was keen on getting in a shopping side trip and they must have found a good store or some great deals. I tilted my head back and closed my eyes. The sun felt good on my face.

"I don't want to intrude. But I saw you here waiting. I couldn't talk to you inside, would be too easy for the rest of the force to eavesdrop. There are rumors that some of the officers may be on the take from the shiners." It was the sergeant from the front desk. "I have someone covering for me for a few minutes so I could come out to talk to you."

I shrugged. "Okay?"

"I saw you on that TV show and loved the episode. You seem like a nice person and Eckart says the local police and you have a good relationship."

"That's true, my aunt is on our small force."

"Well, you didn't hear it from me, but the rumor is the moonshiners are acting up and causing all this trouble. Be careful, they're dangerous and not to be messed with. I'm not sure Eckart would tell you, so I thought I would make sure you know."

"That's kind of you, thanks."

"And, well this is embarrassing. Can I get an autograph for my kid? Her name is Jessica and she would just go nuts if I brought it home to her." He held out a Ghost Hounds t-shirt.

"I'm just a pub owner. You sure you want my John Hancock?"

"You own The Grumpy Chicken. People know it's rumored to be haunted and love the place. Including my daughter. She would really appreciate it. So would I."

I stared at the stern-faced officer with a little girl waiting at home. How could I refuse? He held out a Sharpie ready to go so I signed the shirt and laughed at how bad it came out. I never signed a piece of cloth before. "I'm just a hard working girl that grew up helping my parents run the family business. I'm no TV star, but I hope your daughter enjoys this gift from you."

He gushed, "Thank you." He looked at the signature and ran his hand over it. "By the way, there is one more thing. If you buy moonshine to sell on the side, it's okay, you don't have to tell me. But if you do, be careful. Shiners stick together and if word gets out that you're messing with them, it's not good for you, your business, or your family."

I shuffled my feet to get more comfy. The concrete curb was hard and uncomfortable, but so was this conversation. "It was very nice of you to come out to talk to me and let me know about the moonshiners.

Thank you. And I really hope Jessica likes her t-shirt."

"Oh, I know she is going to love it." He held up the shirt as he spoke.

The horn tooted twice and I saw the powder blue car that belonged to Piper. My two friends waved out of the open windows as the pulled up.

Ida leaned out the passenger window. "Hello officer, you detaining my friend?"

The sergeant chuckled. "No, just the opposite. Asking for a favor. And you can't park there."

Ida waved at me to get in. "We're just picking up Ginger. Not parking. We'll be on our way and you have a nice day."

He nodded. "You too."

I climbed in and we took off. I was in the back seat now next to a pile of bags.

Ida babbled. "We found some good deals at the outlets. You should have seen..." She stopped and you could sense her mind resetting. "But get this. We also found out that Rotgut is out of town."

I cocked my head. "How did you find that out while shopping?"

Piper used her snarkiest voice. "We asked."

"While you were shopping you simply asked

someone?"

Piper continued. "Well, we were looking at the posted menu for a pub in the strip mall we were at. You know, to compare to The Grumpy Chicken's menu when one of the waiters came over to talk to us. He babbled about this and that. But then he bragged 'I can even get a taste of shine for ya if you want'. So I asked if he knew Rotgut."

"Wow. That's kind of amazing but scary too. Seems everyone knows this man."

Ida snorted. "That's what the waiter said, *everyone* knows Rotgut. And he also noted that Rotgut is rumored to be out of town for a while."

I sighed. "Well, nothing went as we thought it would today, but still productive."

Ida twittered. "Yeah, very productive. I got a new pair of pumps at ninety percent off for the awards show!"

I sighed. "Piper, can you pull over so we can drop her at the curb?"

Piper shushed me. "Be quiet. She's in love. And with someone in showbiz. She's having fun. Plus the shoes were a good deal."

"I guess. But we really should pull over at a rest area or someplace so we can swap. I'm doing no good sitting back here with the computers."

Ida spun around. "Just hand it up to me. I'll get back to work." She squinted at me playfully. "Slave driver."

"I deserved that I guess. But we need to know more about Belanger and Brown and the sooner you start the better."

Piper shifted in her seat to look at me in the back seat. "So what did Detective Vader talk to you about?"

"You're not going to believe this. But he tried to help me, told me to be careful because Rotgut is involved."

Ida huffed. "Nothing else?"

"Well, he thought he would be grilling me about the insurance policy, and my finances, but learned more about me after our first meeting and realized he was wrong. And he admitted as much. Then he asked that I keep him informed and not poke around in Savannah. Gave me the usual it's dangerous speech."

Piper turned the radio off then looked in the mirror again. "I've been thinking. We know that someone tried to frame you. So if the insurance policy naming you as beneficiary is a ruse, that means the real money might be changing hands someplace else. And Belanger and Brown both stink like low tide on trash day."

I blinked a few times. "I don't know what low tide on trash day actually smells like, but yes, they're hiding something. That's for sure."

Ida was clicking away on her keyboard and

contributed without looking up, "I'm working on it. They say follow the money, so that's what I'm trying to do. I couldn't find payments from the customer, namely Jacob, to the insurance agency. But maybe I can track it backward. From the agency to the customer."

Piper nodded. "That's pretty clever. Sounds like it should work."

"What else do we need to do with what we learned today?"

Ida cut in. "I need to eat. That pub menu looked really good and we didn't have time to eat lunch. I'm starving."

Piper took the next exit with a blue sign displaying the fork symbol. We found a local diner just off the highway and went inside. It was almost empty and so we had our choice of spots. We took a booth with plenty of room to spread out and work. Ida found an outlet and plugged in her laptop, then talked to her computer screen. "Let's see how good my web crawlers are." She plunked a few keys.

Piper looked over at me. "You alright after meeting with the detective? It was odd to find you sitting on the curb with a cop hovering over you."

"You're not going to believe this, he asked for my autograph, for his daughter."

Piper's jaw hung. "That's so exciting. Piper is dating a cameraman and you're a TV star. Wait, where does that leave me?"

I laughed. "Your a serious journalist. I'm just a waitress slash bartender slash cook. It was silly. But the sergeant also said some of the cops might be taking bribes from the moonshiners. It was strange, but he felt like he needed to warn me about it."

Ida popped. "Holy cow! Look at this. I found a copy of a life insurance policy from Bev Serve. Seems Brown sent it to Belanager. They covered Jacob 'as a key employee to prevent large corporate losses in the untimely event of his death.' The amount is two million dollars. And get this, Jake Belanger is the beneficiary as the owner of Bev Serve."

Piper sat up straight. "The policy that paid to you, Ginger, how much was that for?"

I couldn't stop the reflex and my eyebrows raised as my eyes got bigger. "Fifty-thousand dollars. I thought that was a lot. Till now."

Piper leaned on the table. "Well, well. Would you say two million reasons is enough to call it a motive Ida?"

"For two million, you can use any word you want. That's a lot of money."

I shook my head. "I don't want to seem dumb, but is it legal for a corporation to take a life insurance policy on an employee?"

Piper answered. "I think it is, but there are regulations

that limit its use. And I think Jacob has to sign, too."

I mused. "So if it's regulated, wouldn't it be easier if you had an insurance agent in your pocket?"

Piper smiled. "And the easiest way to get the insurance agent to issue a shady policy, pay him off."

Ida smirked. "Does this mean you're okay letting me hack their bank records?"

My face went long. "No! Not even close. But there has to be an easier, less risky way. I'll bet old Chris Brown has a new boat or some shiny toy in his driveway or garage."

Piper gushed. "Well, now we're getting someplace. We should celebrate a bit, get something nice to eat."

Now it was Ida who had the long face. "No, I'm paying, remember. I can't afford to splurge after buying my new Jimmy Choo pumps. Even if the shoes were on sale."

I teased, "No one made you buy those shoes."

Piper and I laughed, but we resisted the urge to order the more expensive items. Both of us ordered the blue plate special to be considerate to Ida. Our food arrived and we dove in. We reviewed the day's events while we ate and it was still fresh in our minds.

After we finished dinner, we ordered coffee and relaxed, taking some time to unwind. Piper asked, "So, what's next?"

I squinted. "I'm not sure. Belanger may be running some kind of insurance scam. Rotgut is the likely suspect for putting the device on Jacobs car. So the next question in my mind is are they working together? And why?"

Piper replied. "Rotgut makes and sells moonshine. Belanger sells liquor. Do you think Belanger knows him through the business? The waiter said everyone in Savannah knows Rotgut."

I nodded. "That may be true. But *we* don't know Rotgut. We need to get to know him, somehow, and this Belanger guy, too."

Ida asked, "Hey, I meant to ask, but in all the excitement of today, it got lost. Why did you have that large envelope when you came out of the police station?"

"It's for Aunt Mae. Eckart asked that I bring it back from the Savannah station to her."

Piper chuckled. "Ah, so this big meeting was a courier pickup."

I smiled. "You could say that. It all just worked out that way. Like everything else today, it didn't go as expected but we kept things moving forward."

Piper eyed me. "You know when we show up with a package for Deputy Owens from Savannah, everyone is going to know we were sleuthing today. What do we tell everyone back home about what we were doing today?"

"First, we can be discreet with the envelope. And just tell anyone who asks that you came to go shopping and I had a meeting with the detective. It's not a lie, it's just not the whole truth. If we tell them everything, they'll get involved and there is no need for that. We don't need any more people running around, it would just create more problems at this point."

Ida snorted. "Well, we might need some help to learn more about this Rotgut guy. I am starting to get the distinct feeling he doesn't have a big presence on the net."

Piper's eyed twinkled. "So maybe it's time for some old-fashioned work. You know the kind where you look at pieces of paper and talk to actual people."

I smiled. "You miss the good old days, do ya, Piper?"

"No, not really. But every now and then it's nice to get out and read something printed on paper and converse face to face."

Ida huffed. "I converse with people all the time."

Piper shook her head no. "Typing in little boxes on a computer screen doesn't count. Not for this. This man wants to stay out of sight and is not going to let information regarding him slip out. Especially on the internet."

Ida slumped. "You might be right. As far as I can see, he's a ghost."

"So, are we done here? I'm stuffed and ready to get home." I wiped my mouth one last time with the napkin.

Ida sipped her coffee. "No, first you need to see my new shoes!" She sprung out of the booth and sprinted back to the car. She had the shoe box under her arm when she returned. After retaking her seat in the booth, she plunked the box on the table and took the lid off. "Look at those babies."

I had to admit, they were nice shoes. We ended up spending the next hour just chatting, nothing serious just girl talk. It was nice to forget the odd events that consumed us the last few days and just be friends.

Piper finally sat up straight. "Well, this has been fun, but time to go home. Let's roll. I'm ready to get back."

Ida did pay our bill, as promised, and I left a nice tip. I guess I have a soft spot for hard-working waitresses. When I was younger and waiting tables for Mom and Dad, I hated tending a table above and beyond, and then receiving a small tip. I never forgot that lousy feeling and refuse to make someone else feel that way.

We sauntered out and loaded into the car. We were tired but still faced some distance to drive, and then we needed to deal with the gang back home. I had no doubt they would be waiting for our return.

Chapter Eleven

We arrived back at the pub at nine o'clock p.m. I expected a lively crowd, but instead found things calm due to the dwindling people. The dinner crowd was gone and most of the remaining patrons hovered at the bar. Dad tended to them and kept busy wiping glasses while waiting for drink orders. Guardrail, Dog, and Digger sat on their usual stools and Edith and Lily held court at their customary table. The gang occupied their preferred locations, as anticipated, waiting for our return.

We, the three exhausted travelers, trudged for the table next to Lily and Edith. Dog Breath hollered at us as we entered. "Welcome home. The travel team has returned in triumph!"

I stopped to eye the three men perched on stools. "Triumph? How much have you had to drink?"

Guardrail shrugged and bellowed back. "Not much. We're just tired of waiting for ya and we want to know how you made out. And you know Dog has said things far more unusual when he's bored."

Dog Breath retorted with a reflexive, "Hey!" to Guardrail. But it did not deter his enthusiasm and he popped off his perch to dash over to us before we could settle at our table. He left his spot at the bar, beer in hand, to escort us to our seats. "Did you learn anything? I told Guardrail you might even solve this while you were in Savannah." As Dog spoke, he pointed over to the big man on his stool drinking a beer. Digger and Guardrail took that as an invite to come over to the group assembling at the two dining tables.

I locked eyes with the motorcycle mechanic while he took a sip of beer. "Dog, Piper and Ida just went shopping, as evidenced by Ida's new footwear. And I attended a requested meeting with a Savannah based detective. Why do you think we did anything else?"

Dog licked the foam off his upper lip. "You leave without telling anyone why just after what happened to Jacob. Come on, we're smarter than that."

I forced a wry smile. "I love small town life, but I still wish for privacy on many occasions." I crumbled into a seat at the table adjacent to Lily and Edith. Ida and Piper did the same.

Lily said, "Ginger, dear, so who are our suspects?"

Ida placed one hoof on the table. "Look at this beauty! We went shopping I tell ya. No way you'd spot a pair of these in this one horse town."

Lily persisted. "Don't give us that ballyhoo about shopping. We know what you were doing today. We waited for you to come back so we could offer our help."

Dog Breath agreed with an exaggerated nod.

After leaning in my general direction, Edith spoke soft and slow. "Ginger, Beth Givens was here earlier. Spewing all kinds of gossip. She claimed you went to Savannah because you're the prime suspect in Jacob's attack. Said that the police there want to arrest you."

"I'm not surprised. Beth has a gossip gene and would break her neck to spew her falsehoods. I hate it, but right now there's not much I can do about her chatter. So it'll have to wait until tomorrow."

Lily cleared her throat and persisted. "Well, don't make me repeat myself again, who are our suspects?" She emphasized her query by flicking her eyebrows in the universal sign of 'well tell me.'

The gang knew we did some digging into the Jacob mystery, that was clear. And Beth was spreading horrible rumors about me being arrested. So I gave in. "Someone named me as a beneficiary…."

Piper roared. "Hey! Hey! What happened to the plan to be discreet?"

I smiled. "It's clear that was a bad idea and it's better to prevent Beth's false gossip from spreading. Things get so blown out of proportion. We might as well spill the beans and get the truth out."

So I told them the whole story, ending with the dinner meeting held just hours ago. However, I omitted the part concerning Ida's shoes to get to my summary. "This guy Rotgut is bad news and he is the prime suspect for setting the device on Jacob's car. There's also an insurance scam which we think involves Jake Belanger, the owner of Bev Serve, and the insurance salesman, Chris Brown. But we're not sure how the insurance scam and attempt on Jacob are connected. We're assuming Belanger hired Rotgut to murder Jacob, but there is no proof of that."

Dad came over and sat next to me. He kissed my cheek softly. "Sweetie, glad you're home. That's quite a story, but I'm surprised that Jacob's girlfriend isn't of interest."

Ida couldn't resist. "Oh, she's of interest. But for different reasons."

Digger scowled at Ida. "What does that mean?"

"If a fit blonde woman with eyes that literally sparkle, working as an aerobics instructor, intrigues you, then she's of interest." Ida looked down at her own body after she finished.

Guardrail picked up on her tone. "Ah, you got Scooter. You've got nothing to be jealous of. She should be jealous of you." Ida smiled at Guardrail and he returned the gesture. "See and such a pretty smile. So now that that's resolved, what do we do next?"

I whined. "Nooo. I shared the whole story so you would know what's going on. But now you know I'm telling the truth when I say there's not much for us to do. Detective Eckart is all over the insurance scam and every policeman in the state is looking for Rotgut. There is not much we can do but let them do their job."

Digger held his index finger in the air. We all fell quiet and focused on the odd site of the town's gravedigger trying to buzz into the discussion. But it worked, he had the floor. "There may be one thing. I know the moonshiners around here, and they know me. You all know that because I help get shine for The Grumpy Chicken regulars. And you might also know that the mule kick crowd is a pretty tight bunch throughout the south. If there's something going on with this Rotgut character, my friends with stills will know. I can talk with my shine contacts and see what they're hearing."

I pinched the corners of my mouth. "So that would mean meeting with Gator. Is there any chance I could go to that meeting with you?

Digger rubbed his chin. "Maybe. He knows ya. Knows I get the shine for you. So maybe. But the shiners are a pretty jittery bunch."

I nodded. "It'll be alright. Gator watched me grow up here and it shouldn't be a problem. See if you can set it up and let me know when. Thanks." Digger nodded back instead of saying you are welcome. He then took out his phone and fiddled with it.

Dog popped off. "Hey, you know what would be good right about now, some peach pie."

Guardrail waved him off. "No. We have work in the morning. That firewater puts you down for at least a day."

"Yeah, you're right. Just hearing Digger talk about shine made me think, though. Haven't had some in a while and Ginger's peach pie is the only way I like to drink it."

"I know, but can we stay focused, partner." Guardrail patted his business associate on the shoulder and took a seat at Lily and Edith's table. "So, there a few parts to this mystery. Any other theories how they all fit together?"

Piper added, "Everyone seems to think that Jake Belanger hired Rotgut to off Jacob. Then Belanger could collect the two million in insurance money. Rotgut is out of town, assumed to be hiding, which fits if he just attempted to murderer someone. So, this is the most plausible scenario."

Guardrail folded his arms. "That's possible, but it doesn't quite add up to me."

Lily jumped in. "I always say, suspect the lover. And you dismissed his bombshell girlfriend too quickly."

Edith added. "It seems that this insurance policy for two million dollars is a good motive. But why would a successful businessman need to risk his lucrative operation for an insurance scam? That doesn't make sense?"

I nodded. "We agree. We talked about that at dinner. With the operation we saw, this man must be living the good life. Why risk it all?"

Guardrail said, "So there must be more to his story. Maybe he got into debt and is in trouble with a bank, or something."

Ida answered, "No, I looked for large debts. Not only does Jake Belanger seem to be good with business debt, he owns the business outright. No debt and no partners. Same with his home."

Digger grunted. "Well, that's a mega mystery."

Dog Breath laughed. "Well, The Grumpy Gumshoes are good at solving the big mysteries." Dog knew no one liked that name and he fell silent when Piper gave him the stink eye.

I redirected, "Yes, there's a few things to think about, but not much for us to do. But I'm too tired right now to do anything. We told you what we know and that's enough for tonight."

Dad leaned over and whispered to me. "There's one more thing we should talk about."

Bones burst through the swinging door from the kitchen and hollered. "Alright, all the dishes are clean and the prep station is empty and sanitized. Time for me to get in on things! Ginger, did you hear?"

I threw my hands in the air. "Hear what? That Beth was gossiping?"

Bones spoke rapidly. "No! Star came over to talk with you this afternoon. But you weren't here so she had a brief chat with Dixie. While they were talking, Star fell into a trance and saw the grumpy chicken. When Dixie shook her out of it, Star told her about a weird vision. Then Dixie saw a strange rash, or more like a tattoo, form on Star's palm. Dixie flipped out and Tom sent her home for the day."

I glanced around. "That makes no sense. But I was wondering where Dixie was."

Dad sighed. "I didn't want you to hear it like that." He glared at Bones for a second. "But Dixie was pretty upset. Or maybe it's more like..."

Bones jumped in. "It's more like she was freaking out. Dixie was ranting and she said Star was so cold that she felt like ice."

Dad waved his hand at Bones. "The boy is exaggerating. Dixie was understandably excited and we're still not sure what happened."

Bones continued. "I don't know. Dixie was pretty shook up."

I sat up straight. "Seems the travel crew wasn't the only ones that had an interesting day." I looked at Dad. "So who made drinks when Dixie went home early?"

Dad huffed. "You seem to forget I took care of this bar long before you were born. I can still pull a beer and shake a drink better than any man alive."

I laughed. "I know. But that's why you were a little

slow to come over. And this quiet demeanor is a bit out of character for you. You're tired."

Dad stuck his nose in the air. "Maybe, but at my age, I have that right." Then he huffed. I put my arm around his shoulder and gave him a sideways hug. He smiled back at me.

Guardrail whispered to me. "Don't let him tend bar again. He would only serve Guinness. We kept telling him we wanted a pilsner. But he said that's not a proper beer and ignored us and gave us that thick, brown stuff."

I looked back at him. "I'm sorry, I'll make it up to you."

Bones continued, "So what do you think that was all about with Dixie and Star?"

I waved my hand in front of my face. "Not now. I'll talk to Dixie and Star. Hear their versions of the story. But tomorrow. I'm tired just like Dad."

Bones insisted. "I just told you exactly what happened."

I forced a smile. "I know, Bones, I believe you. But I have some questions for Dixie and Star after hearing that story. It will just have to wait until morning, after I get some requisite sleep. I'm done for today, good night." I kissed my Dad on the cheek, rose from my seat, and made a beeline for the apartment. I was dog-tired and it was painfully obvious that I had another long day ahead of me tomorrow.

Chapter Twelve

Six a.m. came fast and the cell phone demanded attention. I woke from my sound sleep but let it ring to voice mail. After a brief pause, it rang again. I picked up my flip-phone and opened it. I moved my mouth but nothing came out, so I cleared my throat. "Hello, who is this? It better be important." The gravely voice that came out of the earpiece surprised me.

"Ginger, it's Digger. You didn't respond to the text I sent late last night so I had to call you this morning. Gator can meet you at the old church at seven. Get up and get dressed, you don't want to be late. He doesn't like to wait."

"Thanks, I think. I didn't expect to meet Gator on such short notice, but okay. I want to talk to him."

"I understand. I'm surprised, too. I sent him a text last night when we were talking. I was surprised when he responded late last night. He doesn't usually do that and he must want to talk to you, too."

"Great, well I need to go then so I can get ready. I'll meet you at the old church at seven. See ya then, bye Digger." I closed my phone.

I knew Gator, but while showering I could feel some nerves forming. He is a Potter's Mill native but he keeps a low profile and I rarely saw him in the pub. Moonshiners are a private lot and the number of actual conversations I had with the man could be counted on two hands. Now he wanted to talk to me.

I threw on the same bluejeans from yesterday and a clean t-shirt. Then I added a green long-sleeved button-down shirt for warmth. The morning dew would make things feel cool down at Bear's Paw Hill.

I put my red hair back in a pony tail, no time for anything fancy, and grabbed my cell phone. Then I tiptoed to the back door to keep from waking Dad, eased the door open and closed it gently, then I was off.

It was chilly. But the cool air and the walk to Bear's Paw Hill woke me fully. I was aware and thinking clearly now. I loved this beautiful walk. The old church was built on the hilltop next to Bear's Paw swamp. You could see it from quite a distance as you approached and the white building with it's big steeple was picturesque. In fact, it was snapped by the shutter bug tourists as much as the old mill on the river. I even think the general store sells post cards with the church's image.

My mind wandered to Jacob. As I hiked up the hill I made a mental note to visit him later in the day. My old beat up Volkswagen Beetle was on it's last legs, but it should be able to get me out to the regional hospital, and then back, one more time.

My thoughts then jumped to the mystery of why

would a successful businessman set up an insurance scam that risked everything. And what is the connection between Brown and Belanger? We assumed the insurance guy, Brown, was paid off, but he was taking a big risk, too. Then there was the question of the link between Belanger and Rotgut. And how did Jacob fit into all of this? I realized that pieces to this puzzle did not fit well because we were still missing too many parts. My racing mind kept me engrossed and I lost track of where I was. I knew because I stood in front of the old church in what seemed like no time at all. Somehow I was early, maybe I power walked while lost in thought.

The raspy voice came from the corner of the church. "Ginger, over here." It was Digger.

I moved toward the sound of his voice to find him and Gator waiting for me in the shadow of the church. They were early too. I nodded and said, "Good morning gentlemen. I appreciate you getting up so early to meet."

Gator was what most people think of as a stereotypical Southerner. He always wore old-fashioned overalls and chewed tobacco. The receding gray hair did not go well with the large belly and the round face sporting a long gray beard, like a ZZ Top band member. And then there was the drawl. It was so thick that even I, a girl born and raised in Georgia, could not understand him at times. Moonshiners were hardened by working illegal stills in the dark of night, deep in the woods, and the demands of this work showed on Gator's face. His smooth, deep voice did not match the crusty exterior.

"Ginger, I got Digger's text last night and wanted to speak to you immediately after learning you're poking into Rotgut's business."

"Thanks."

"Don't thank me. Listen. You need to stop. I'm hearing rumors that Rotgut has gone off the rails. That he got stiffed on a deal and lost wheelbarrows of money. He's fighting mad and will stop at nothing to get his own form of justice." He put a wad of chewing tobacco in his cheek.

I nodded in agreement. "We think he's the one to wire Jacob's car in an attempt to kill him."

"That's what this man does. He leaves a path of destruction wherever and whenever he feels threatened. He'll not flinch to kill you and everyone in that pub of yours if he thinks you're messing with his business."

"So I hear."

Gator spit on the ground and glared at me. "You need to be quiet and listen hard to what I'm saying. Me and the other shiners are keeping clear of the man. Too dangerous for our business since every cop in the state is looking for him. To boot, we're afraid of what he might do if he panics. If me and my pals are afraid, you need to be too. Stay clear of the man. I've seen you grow from a girl to a woman. I would hate to see ya get hurt. So listen to what I'm telling you." Gator had a look of sadness as he finished talking. Then he added, "I hate that Rotgut is part of the white lightening business." He spit at the thought. "We got enough problems keeping the stills hidden and producing quality hooch without a madman making us look worse."

"I get it. Thanks for the warning. I have a question for you."

Digger was keeping watch while we talked, but he turned to look at me when heard my question. "Ginger, keep it short."

"I will Digger. Gator, I saw lots of copper on the electrical device wired into Jacob's Mustang. The shiners use lots of copper, right?"

"Copper is used for the boilers, condensers, piping, all kinds of parts, yes. Doesn't corrode and it's soft enough to work with. We can cut it, shape it with basic tools out in the woods."

"So a moonshiner would have copper laying around?"

"Of course. Copper is used all the time."

"How about electrical things, like switches and relays?"

"I don't use that stuff, but some of the more modern stills are getting automated. But only the ones that have electricity. My stills are deep in the woods. There's no electricity, so no reason for me to worry about electrical gadgets. But I heard Rotgut pays off the cops in Savannah and has some stills in remote warehouses that do run on electricity. So if your asking if he uses gadgets like that, maybe. Now stop asking questions and forget about all this. It's more dangerous than you can imagine. Open your pub, enjoy your customers. You're a good girl and I hate the thought of you crossing paths with Rotgut."

Digger pleaded with his eyes. "Listen to Gator. He's trying to help you."

Gator spit again. "Digger was my best friend growing up. And he always gave me good advice. I suggest you listen to both of us. Stay out of this. It you don't, not just you will get hurt, but so will those you love like Tom."

I pinched my lips, and sighed. "I know you came here promptly out of concern or worry and it was not easy or convenient to get out here this early. So thanks. Digger is a good friend to both of us for setting this up, and I appreciate both of you taking this time."

Gator chuckled. "I'm worried, yes. But that's 'cause I don't want to give the police any reason to start scouring the woods for Rotgut. So I have my own concerns about the fallout of your meddling. Don't read too much into this. It's just business."

I nodded and kept quiet. Digger smiled too then asked. "Are we done?"

Gator held his hand up. "No, one more thing. I need to get that recipe for your peach pie. I keep hearing the boys like what you do with my shine. How you dress it up."

I laughed. "It's pretty easy to do. Takes the bite out of the raw ruckus juice. Makes it go down easier."

Gator cocked his head. "My shine is as smooth as it gets! But I understand, I guess. The liquor most people buy these days is so weak in comparison. They're not used to it. It's why I whip up some peach or apple pie of my own from time to time. Some of my customers prefer it that way, but they tell me your peach pie is the best."

I wanted to ask so many more questions about Rotgut and was frustrated that Gator was talking to me about liquor recipes. I suppressed the urge to ask for more information. "I can ask Dixie to write it down. It's actually her recipe. I think she will share it. But you know Dixie."

Gator laughed. "Yes, I do. Everyone who grew up here knows Dixie is, let's say, a little excitable. But she knows me and tell her I'll make it worth her while."

I smiled at the two men. They did not have to do this. But both knew it is what we do, the right thing to do, in our small town. We protected each other. I reached my hand out to Gator. "I won't forget you took this time and your show of consideration. Come by the pub sometime, I'll get you the recipe and a glass of my peach pie to try."

Digger scanned the area. I realized for the first time how jumpy he was acting. Gator must have seen me studying our lookout and he ignored the handshake I tried to initiate. He said, "See, Digger gets it. Rotgut on the warpath means we all have to be on our toes, all the time. Till this blows over."

I put my hand back at my side and pressed my luck. "Do you have any idea where Rotgut is?"

Gator frowned. "If I did, I would turn him in to the cops myself. Like I said, men like him are bad for men like me working with covert stills."

I think my cheeks blushed a little. "Sorry, had to ask. It would eat at me all day if I didn't."

"It's okay. I understand. You were always a curious little girl. But make that the last time you wonder about where he is. It will get you killed if you don't." Gator turned and made his way towards the swamp. Apparently, he did not like to repeat himself.

I raised my voice a little so he could hear. "Can you let me know if you hear Rotgut is seen in the area." Gator shook his head no and kept walking. He didn't even turn to look back. We were done.

Chapter Thirteen

I was full of energy after the early morning walk and clandestine meeting. On returning to The Grumpy Chicken, I jumped right into the days work and completed much of my to do list. At around nine o'clock, I started prepping twenty pounds of beef for the day's special, shaved steak sandwiches. While chopping the meat with my well worn chef's knife, I mulled the upcoming talk with Dixie and Star. What were the right questions to ask about the odd incident?

The knock on the front door was firm and loud. Someone desired in to The Grumpy Chicken early, so I went to the front entrance and flipped the deadbolt. I found Sheriff Morrison waiting on the other side. "Hey! Good morning, Ginger. Can I come in? I have something to talk to you about."

"Good morning to you, too. Sure."

We made our way through the dining room and back into the kitchen. We made small talk on the short walk, then I picked up the knife and went back to work while the Sheriff said, "Ginger, there's news concerning Jacob. He came out of the coma."

I put the knife down and rested both hands on the cutting board. "What? When?"

"About three-thirty this morning."

"Is he okay?"

"The doctors are doing tests to figure that out. But he talked a little. So I went out to the regional hospital, to question him while he was awake."

"That's kind of harsh. Poor guy comes out of a coma in the middle of the night and you questioned him first thing?"

"I hate it too, honest. But I couldn't risk him lapsing back into a coma without getting some answers."

"So, did you?"

"Yeah, it's why I am here, to let you know."

"I don't like the sound of that."

The Sheriff smiled. "No, it's fine. I'm actually doing you a favor, not bringing bad news."

"That's good."

"Look, I asked him about the policy that named you as a beneficiary. He said he had no idea what it was or who bought it. He knew no more than you do."

"Well, that's interesting."

"See. I'm trying to be more of a friend, not the Sheriff right now."

"I appreciate that and now I feel bad you got a call in the middle of the night to go all the way out there."

"It's all part of the job. This part is kind of sensitive, and I'm not sure I should tell you. But here goes. When I asked Jacob about the mysterious insurance policy, he acknowledged that he still loved you but he was adamant that he did not buy the policy. He insisted there is no reason to do something that strange and was unaware of why someone would buy a policy like that. You and I know that someone might be trying to frame you for the attempted murder and it was probably someone like this Rotgut character. However, Jacob has no idea of what is going on, I'm sure of that after talking to him."

"I'm not sure how to respond to all that. But I appreciate you sharing with me. That's actually touching he acknowledged his feelings for me. He's not much of a romantic and doesn't share his inner emotions well. It's one of the reasons we drifted apart."

"I hope I didn't upset you. I really don't want that. But if there's anything that comes to mind after hearing this, I need to know. We know quite a bit about this case, but there are a few pieces still missing. This is..."

In what felt like deja vu, a similar knock emanated from the front door repeating the same firm and loud blows heard just minutes ago. I excused myself and returned to the entrance and flipped the bolt once more. This time it was Aunt Mae standing there.

She came in and kissed me on the cheek. I returned

the peck. "What is it with you police? You all knock the same. Hard and loud."

Aunt Mae chuckled. "They actually teach us that as part of our training."

"Well, who would have guessed." I smiled, glad to see her. We headed to the kitchen to join the Sheriff, who I left unattended. Aunt Mae laughed when she saw him. "You beat me here."

The Sheriff stood upright and acted nonchalant when he heard us, but I caught a quick glimpse of him scrutinizing the cutting board. He mumbled, "Yep. Looks that way."

I smiled at Sheriff Morrison. "You checking to see if I can shave steak thin with a knife?"

"No, well, yes. The steak looks good and I might come by for lunch."

I chuckled. "I hope you do."

Mae looked at the Sheriff. "I see you were going over the important business of the day – lunch. I came over because I need to pick up the package Eckart sent us. But I was also going to tell Ginger about Jacob coming out of the coma. So why are you really here so early."

The Sheriff sighed. "I'm not good at this and I'm not related to Ginger, like you. But I interviewed Jacob and I thought she should hear it from me directly."

Aunt Mae tilted her head to one side and squinted slightly. "That's so sweet. Especially since you did something nice and it wasn't for those stinky horses."

He pulled a faux stern face. "Careful when you bring up my mounts." Then he smiled. "So how did you find out?"

"Leonard was on duty last night and got the initial call from the hospital."

He snorted. "Well, I need to talk with Deputy Wise about his use of discretion."

Mae smiled at the Sheriff. "In any case, this was really nice of you to come over and talk with Ginger."

He fiddled with his radio. "Well, I think we're just about done and I was about to leave. I was saying, Ginger, if you think of anything, let me know immediately. I would appreciate it and it may help us. Even if it seems trivial."

I cleared my throat. "Before you go, I do have a question for both of you. We found that Bev Serve took out a life insurance policy on Jacob for two million dollars. Is that legal for an employer to take out a life insurance policy on an employee?"

The Sheriff shot lasers from his eyes. "How do you know that?"

"Looks like you know about it, too. I'm guessing it's another reason why you jumped at the chance to confirm what Jacob really knows."

The Sheriff tilted his back. "Good guess. And no miss smarty pants, it's not legal unless it's signed by the person insured by the company."

"Did Jacob know anything about the Bev Serve policy?"

The Sheriff shook his head no.

I sighed. "That means someone had to forge Jacob's signature then. So who took out the policy and why?"

Aunt Mae answered. "That's what we we are trying to figure out and why we've been burning the midnight oil. Well, that and trying to find the moonshiner we suspect set the device up on Jacob's starter."

I looked at the floor for a second. "I met the insurance agent in Savannah and it is obvious he is no criminal mastermind. But he's involved in some way, I'm sure of that. So the owner of Bev Serve could have been the one who dreamed all this up. But he must be smart to run such a big business. Did whoever took out the insurance policies think no one could figure it out?"

Sheriff Morrison said, "Detective Eckart is one of the best when it comes to financial crimes. So that was a mistake if he did. Eckart sniffed out the questionable insurance policies in less than forty-eight hours."

I snorted. "I don't know how he gets anything done, that police station is a zoo."

Aunt Mae grinned. "It's not Potter's Mill for sure, but they have *lots* of resources there."

"If they have lots of resources, why haven't they been able to arrest this Rotgut guy then. It sounds like he's a bad dude that belongs behind bars. Everything points at him as the suspect for setting the device on Jacob's car. And he was probably hired by Jake Belanger at Bev Serve."

The Sheriff rocked his head. "I agree, I wish we had him in custody. But some guys are good at covering their tracks and we have to have evidence to arrest a person or the prosecutors just let them go without filing charges. And after the attempt on Jacob, Rotgut became a ghost. No one has seen him or knows where he is."

Aunt Mae frowned. "Rotgut has been hiding in the shadows but we will get him soon. I promise."

The Sheriff jumped in again. "I don't know about the soon part Deputy Owens, but we want him behind bars and the sooner the better. Yes."

I blinked a few times as the memory of the envelope popped. "Aunt Mae, before I forget, I have to get the envelope for you."

She nodded. "That's the second reason I'm here. Detective Eckart said you would have a package for me and the Sheriff."

"Can I ask what it is?"

The Sheriff's voice took his best official tone. "You can ask, but we won't tell you."

It was time for Dixie and Bones to arrive so I wasn't surprised to hear someone unlock the front door and come in. Dixie's blaring voice confirmed who it was. "If you're still here, please leave. Now! I don't need some deformed ghost chicken bothering me while I work."

The Sheriff looked at me like an incontinent dog in a room filled with fire hydrants. He sputtered. "I'm not sure what that's all about with Dixie. But I'm pretty sure it's my cue to leave."

"See ya around. Aunt Mae, can you keep Dixie company while I go get the envelope upstairs?"

Sheriff Morrison let himself out and Aunt Mae nodded, then headed to the bar to talk with Dixie. I made for the apartment to retrieve the envelope and complete my courier mission.

I returned with package under my arm. Aunt Mae and Dixie were chit chatting. I noticed Mae raiding the condiment tray, popping a few olives in her mouth. "Auntie, that's not a very good breakfast."

Aunt Mae flinched. "This incident with Jacob has kept everyone hopping. The Savannah police have pulled out all the stops trying to find Rotgut and they have enlisted our help. I have to eat what I can, when I can. And I love your olives."

I laughed. "I know. Dixie, you alright? I heard what

happened yesterday."

"I'm fine. But I'm for sure tired of that plucking grumpy chicken making unannounced appearances."

"I heard he didn't appear, but that Star saw it in a vision."

Dixie nodded. "Yeah. You should've seen it. The ice tea I gave her froze, solid. And she was cold, too. Real cold to the touch when I shook her awake."

"Then what?"

"Star told me she saw the grumper in a hazy vision. The chicken led Star into a wooded area and she saw a scary man yelling at someone. Something about a deal gone bad and losing over a million dollars."

Aunt Mae raised her eyebrows. "That would make me upset, too. That's a lot of money."

Dixie continued, "But it didn't stop there. I gave Star some hot coffee to warm her up and then I noticed it forming. A mark on her palm. It appeared slowly, and was faint at first, but then became clear in green, like a tattoo."

Aunt Mae asked, "So, what did it look like?"

Dixie paused. "The symbol was weird like everything else. It was two crossed arrows. But one of the arrows was broken in half."

I looked at Aunt Mae and she grimaced. It was weird,

yes, but it made no sense to any of us. "Auntie, I think I need to go see Star. She might understand this a little better than we do." I held out the envelope.

She nodded and took the package. "Sounds like a good idea. I have work to do back at the station. I'll talk to ya later."

Dixie and I said goodbye to Aunt Mae and she left. I decided to leave the rest of the prep work for Bones. The morning's events altered my priorities and I needed to talk with Star, without delay.

Chapter Fourteen

I stood at the front door of the new age store rapping hard and loud. The slight movement of the closed sign with each knock made me realize I was banging just like the Sheriff and Aunt Mae. But it worked. I saw her through the big glass door and she rushed to answer. She opened the door. "Good morning, Ginger. What's all the commotion?"

"I'm sorry, but I really need to talk with you."

She smiled. "Of course, come on in."

We made our way to the large table in the center of the store. The fancy cloth covering made it feel homey but the crystal ball in the center was a bit much, in my opinion. However, Star believed in its power and I respected her convictions. We both sat and she pushed some papers to one side then looked at me. "So what can I do for you?"

"Well, I heard about the incident yesterday and I have some questions."

"It was incredible, the most vivid vision I've ever had. And I saw your chicken. She has beautiful white feathers with black and red accents. I felt a gentle spirit, kind and loving. But one of her legs is injured."

"That's interesting, but Dixie also said you saw a man

in the woods. What did he look like? Did you recognize him?"

"No, I never saw him before. But he was mean looking, downright ugly. And he was yelling at someone about a deal gone bad. Said he lost over a million dollars."

I felt myself gasp at the amount of money. "Did you see the other man, the one the awful man was talking to?"

"No."

"Dixie also said you had a mark appear in one palm. Is it still there?"

Star held out her left palm. "No, see? It went away after twenty-minutes."

"What did it look like?"

Star shuffled in a pocket and took out her phone. "I knew it was important so I took a picture." She opened the file and handed the phone to me.

I took the phone and the mark was more like a sketch of two crossed arrows, but one arrow was clearly broken in half. I asked, "Do you know what this means?"

"Not at first. But I remembered after a while that two crossed arrows represent friendship in some Indian tribes. But the broken arrow is unusual."

"So is there any explanation for why one arrow would

be broken?"

"Well, I thought about that for a while. Then I wondered if the bad deal mentioned in my vision was connected. And it hit me, the one arrow may represent a break in the friendship. And a transaction involving a loss like a million dollars, that could break almost any friendship."

"Holy limpin' chicken! It couldn't be. The marking color was green, wasn't it?" I saw Star nod yes, and continued, "Green like money?"

"Yes."

"Could that also mean the friendship was broken over money?"

Star gasped. "I didn't think about it, but now that you mention it, sure. And the image was on my left palm, the palm that itches when money is being paid out, or lost."

"Star, hang on I need to make a call." I took my phone out and called Ida. She answered on the second ring. "Ida, I need a big favor. Can you print out pictures of Rotgut and Jake Belanger, then bring them over to Star's new age shop?"

Ida stammered a moment. "This is a bit unusual, but I guess. Be there in ten or fifteen." She clicked off. Star shared some scones bought for breakfast while we waited for Ida. I looked at Star. "Have you ever had a mark like that on you before?"

"No. It's very rare. That's why I took a picture. And I was thinking about why a mark after a vision? Dixie woke me before the vision was complete. At least it felt that way to me. So if that is the case, maybe the spirit, in this instance your chicken, left the mark to make sure I got the message."

I snorted at the ridiculous thought. "You're saying the chicken not only tried to communicate, it tried to help you when you were brought out of the trance early?"

"Yes, spirits help us all the time."

I failed to contain a brief chuckle and then my face went blank when the memory hit me. "There was this one time where I saw initials in some brining chicken wings. Now that I think about it, it was kind of similar to your palm mark."

The knock at the front door was soft and we almost missed it. Star went to let Ida in and the two returned to the table. Star took her seat. Ida fought to catch her breath as she took a laptop bag off her shoulder and hung it on her chair. "I need to get some exercise. I think I sit at the keyboard too much." Ida sat.

I chuckled. "You think?"

Ida snapped at me. "Hey, I'm trying to do you a favor here."

"I know, but we really should make sure you get more exercise. Did you bring the pictures?"

"Of course." Ida plunked down a piece of paper with two pictures on it. "Even printed it out on my color printer."

I took the paper and slid it over to Star. "Either of these men the one you saw in your vision?"

Star went white. "This one." She put her finger on Rotgut's mug. "I will never forget his ugly face. And how mean he was."

Ida blurted out. "What's going on here? She saw Rotgut? So where is he? Everyone is looking for him."

I was lost in thought, but tried to calm Ida. "Do you remember when we heard about the vision Star had last night? Rotgut was the man in her vision."

"That moonshiner just keeps popping up, doesn't he?

I felt a chill run through my body. "We need to get to the hospital. Jacob is danger. I know what's going on."

Ida squeaked. "What in the world are talking about?"

"Jacob is in danger. Everyone is thinking Rotgut tried to kill him because Belanger hired him. But that's not it. Rotgut got double crossed by Belanger, that is what the palm mark meant. And Jacob might have been involved with the deal. Remember the 'big deal' Jacob mentioned in one email? You found that early on, Ida. And this morning, Gator told me Rotgut was mad because he lost a large sum of money. It all fits."

Ida gawked at the moonshiner's picture. "You're right. And a man like Rotgut would hunt them down for sure, make them pay."

"Jacob needs protection and we need to find Belanager. I don't think he's out town on business. I think he's on the run."

Star asked, "How are we going to do all that?"

I reached into the pocket of my jeans. "We can't by ourselves. But I know how to get some help." I plunked Detective Eckart's card down on the tablecloth and pulled out my phone. I dialed the handwritten number on the back and the detective answered on the first ring. I explained what we pieced together and he was skeptical at first, but I could tell his instincts told him this made sense.

It was prudent to take action and he said, "S.O.P. is we post one uniformed officer on a victim's room after an attempt. But that won't be enough if Rotgut is coming for Jacob."

"How fast can reinforcements get there?"

Eckart mulled, "I think it's best if we move him. I can have him transferred to a more secure location in about an hour. In the meantime, I'll have Jacob moved to an undisclosed room until they move him out of that hospital."

"Okay. And what about Belanger?"

Eckart snorted. "I thought I had a meeting next week with him. He told me he was out of town on business. But I think you're right. He used that line as cover to get some time to run. I spoke to him on the phone a day ago. I am tracking the towers used for his calls to see if I can pin point where he is. My gut has been telling me something is off with him since day one."

"Do you need me to do anything?"

"Not that I can think of. Look, I've got lots to do here now. If you find anything else, let me know. I need to go. Thanks, Ginger." He clicked off.

I looked up to find Star and Ida staring at me, waiting for information. I replied, "Help is on the way for Jacob. He'll be moved to a new secret location."

Ida sighed. "Wow, I never thought I would worry about your ex. I'm relieved to hear that."

Star shuddered. "Be careful. Something is still off. I sense danger."

"What's that supposed to mean?" Ida was a tad blunt.

Star smiled back. "That's how it is sometimes with the spirits. They give me a general feeling, but nothing more. But I have found it is always wise to pay attention to the inklings they give me. I may misinterpret them sometimes, but in hindsight, they're always right."

Ida looked at me. "That gave me the willies. How about you?"

"Yeah. But for some reason I fully understand what she's saying. Star, thank you. This was helpful and you may have saved Jacob. How can I repay you?"

"You're welcome. And if you're serious, I would appreciate it if you agreed to the dinner seance."

I looked down and took a deep breath. "Alright. We can do a dress rehearsal. Just friends and family. Work out all the kinks before doing it with the general public."

Star smiled. "That sounds fair enough."

Ida thumped the table with her hand. "Well, what do we do now?."

"I'm not sure. But I don't think we can just sit around and wait. Thanks again Star. We'll see ya soon."

Ida grabbed her computer bag off the chair back and Star waved goodbye. We were off for the short walk one door over to The Grumpy Chicken.

Chapter Fifteen

Ida and I made haste for the pub. The visit with Star produced unexpected results and I wanted to make sure we didn't miss something. Plus, Belanger and Rotgut remained at large and we needed to find them. Talking with the gang would allow us to review things, maybe spark a new thought, and help us identify the next steps. The police were on it, but if we could help resolve the case in a more timely fashion, the sooner I would breath easy.

In the excitement, though, I forgot the time. Upon entering The Grumpy Chicken, the place was empty. It was still morning, albeit late morning, and we had just opened for the early lunch crowd. The gang would not be at the bar till noon, at the earliest.

Dixie saw us and hollered. "Well, did you learn anything?"

I snorted. "And then some. You won't believe it."

Dixie shot back, "Try me."

"Rotgut is actually hunting down Jacob and the owner of Bev Serve, this Belanger guy. Belanger reneged on a deal with Rotgut, costing the shiner over a million."

Dixie stood up straight. "Ouch! That's not pocket change. So how did you figure that out?"

"The grumper. The vision and mark Star experienced told a story. Then we figured out what it meant. I called Eckart in Savannah and he is having Jacob moved for protection."

"Specter connector! Are you admitting to me the grumpy chicken helped you piece this together?"

I chuckled. "I'm not sure." I stopped and shook my head trying to rid the thought. But the notion stayed and I had to be honest. "Check that. Yeah. Our grumpy friend helped figure this out."

Dixie let out a belly laugh. "Oh man, I can't wait to tell Tom. See his face when he hears about this."

"That's not all either. I know what's going on with the insurance policies. If Belanger robbed Rotgut through some sort of scam, then he would have to leave Savannah forever. The company insurance policy he bought for Jacob as a 'key' employee was for two million. Between that and the over one million stolen from Rotgut, he would be set for life. He can live wherever he wants. But he needed time to collect the insurance money and then get away. That is where the second fake life insurance policy comes in. You know, the one made to look like Jacob bought it and names me as the beneficiary? It frames me for the murder giving Belanger time to collect his three million and flee."

Dixie and Ida looked like their brains ached. Dixie erupted. "What in the blazes are you cackling about. The cats that sneak in here make more sense than you do right now."

I persisted. "Belanger made sure Jacob handled this 'big deal' with Rotgut. So when Belanger stole the money from the Rotgut deal, over a million dollars, he knew Rotgut would kill Jacob. With Jacob' death, the two million life insurance policy would pay Belanger. But that would take time. So he used another fake policy, framing me, as a smoke screen to get that time."

Ida cocked her head. "Oh, that makes more sense, sure."

I stomped my foot. "It's a bit complicated, I know. It takes a minute to settle in and make sense. But it all fits together perfectly."

Dixie chuckled. "So Belanger tricked Rotgut to commit a murder that he needed done to collect insurance money?"

"Yeah. But it was clever how he tricked Rotgut with a phony deal to set it all up, then stole the moonshiner's money as a bonus."

Dixie's jaw hung. "This was Jacob's boss? Wow! Makes you look good in comparison, Ginger."

I pulled a fake hurt face. "Ha, ha, very funny."

Ida shook her head no. "We can't let this Belanger creep get away. He sets all this up, then sits back and collects the money. Meanwhile, Rotgut gets his hands dirty and Jacob gets killed. That's pure evil."

I added, "Eckart is trying to track Belanger down right

now. Thinks maybe he can use the cell towers to find him."

The front door opened. It was Piper and she stopped a few steps in sensing that something was going on. "Alright, out with it. What happened?"

We told her the news and like Ida, Piper quickly labeled Belanger evil. We continued to discuss the recent events and there was sense of excitement to it all. Another mystery to solve and solve we did. At least I hoped so.

Bones whipped up some shaved steak sandwiches, cut them into bite size chunks, then put toothpicks in each piece. I was shocked that my young dishwasher/grill cook actually made a nice hors-d'oeuvre out of a simple steak sandwich. He was more creative than any of us knew.

At noon, Guardrail came in with Dog Breath in tow. They smelled the steak cooking on the grill and Dog raised his nose in the air, taking in a good whiff. "Haven't had shaved steak on the menu for a while. Smells real good."

Guardrail smiled. "I agree. Makes me realize how hungry I am. Might even get a cold beer even though I don't usually drink at lunch."

Dog added, "Some sandwiches scream for cold beer. And shaved steak is one of them." He smacked his hands together, then rubbed them like he was trying to generate a spark.

Bones made lunch for the custom motorcycle mechanics and Dixie poured two beers for them. While the boys waited for their sandwiches, the town spinsters wandered in. Edith nudged her older sister. "See, I told you, Lily. It was a good idea to come here for lunch. Things are happening and that means the gang will be in the pub."

Lily popped back. "It's not the gang until we're here!" The two elderly sisters laughed at her comment.

The door swung open again, this time it was Digger. He saw the spinster sisters laughing. "What's so funny? You laughing at me?"

Edith spun around. "There you are Digger, glad you made it. Seems the gang's assembling."

They all took seats and ordered something to eat. I noshed on Bone's hors-d'oeuvres plate and after an hour of chit chat, my phone rang. It was a blocked number. "Hello?"

"Ginger? It's Detective Eckart."

"I thought it was your voice. We were just talking about Jacob's..."

"Listen, this is important and I'm short for time. There was an incident when we moved Jacob. One of our uniforms thought he saw a suspicious pickup truck as they were leaving. When he went to check it out, he identified the driver as Rotgut. They chased him for a while but he got away. Rotgut *is* hunting Jacob, like you thought, but he could also be hunting others. I think it's wise if you keep a low profile. Maybe even have your Aunt come over for a while."

"Thanks for telling me. I'll call my aunt but she is swamped with everything going on..."

"Then I'll call her. She'll listen to a fellow officer. Rotgut is the worst of the worse. We can't be too cautious. I got to go, they might have found something with Belanger's phone. Bye." He clicked off.

I felt my face droop. "That's not the call I was hoping for. They spotted Rotgut hunting for Jacob as they moved him to a new hospital. Even chased him for a bit but he got away."

Dixie gulped. "So do they have an idea of where Rotgut might be heading?"

"Nope. And that is what Eckart is concerned about. Says we should be careful."

Piper motioned no with her head. "He's not coming here. We had nothing to with stealing Rotgut's money. He has no reason to come here."

But Piper was wrong. The front door flew open and a large man entered. My brain refused the first data sent from my eyes. But it registered after a second. I was staring at Rotgut cradling a shotgun.

Chapter Sixteen

We stared at the hulk standing in front of us. Rotgut was almost as big as Guardrail, but he looked tens time larger with the shotgun nestled in one arm. I heard his voice for the first time. "Alright. This is the place Jacob Allen did business at the day before he was hurt. Who did he meet with?" No one moved or said a word. He raised his voice. "I'll say it again. Who did he meet with?"

Dixie flinched, just a little, and Rotgut pounced. "So, you must be the one he met with?"

Dixie whimpered. "I was here when he called on us, yes. But I'm just the bartender I only made the list of stuff we needed."

Rotgut came over and stood right in front of me. "You must be his ex-wife. He said you had red hair. And yours is the only red hair on a woman in here."

I felt fear flash through my body like a jolt of electricity. But I reached deep and stood up straight. "I am. And I did meet with Jacob."

"Well, now we're getting somewhere. Where's my money? And where did the pigs take him?"

I looked at him like I was seeing a horse riding a man. "What makes you think I know anything about where the police took Jacob? And I don't know anything about your money. So why you asking me?"

"Because Jacob came here after he ripped me off. To his ex-wife's place. This little town makes a great place to be on the lamb. And with an ex to help, it's perfect."

"Jacob came to sell me liquor and beer. That's all. I didn't even have dinner with him."

"So you're telling me that your ex came all the way out here to the country only to sell some beer to ya?"

"Yes. Nothing more."

Rotgut's face turned bright red. He roared, "I hate being lied to! Tell me where my money is and where they took Jacob!"

My knees tried to buckle as his voice hit me like a tidal wave. I was surprised to find I was still standing. "I don't know. I'm telling you the truth."

This was a real bad time for Dog Breath to find his voice, but he did. "Listen, I know you don't know that lady like I do. But if she tells you it's the truth or she doesn't know something, you can take it to the bank. She is not capable of lying."

Rotgut stormed over to the stool occupied by the Vietnam veteran sporting a gray ponytail. He went nose to nose with Dog Breath and studied the lines on his face. Then Rotgut shifted his shotgun and jammed the butt of it into Dog's stomach. Dog Breath crumbled to the floor.

"Anyone else want to open their mouth?" Rotgut paced the dining room. Then he stopped about ten-feet in front of me. "Good!" He focused back on me. "So, you had a minute to think a little. Now, pretty lady, did you remember where my money is or where they took your useless ex-husband?"

"I don't know anything about either of those things."

Rotgut carried the shotgun like a hunter, cradled in one of his arms, pointed diagonally to the sky. But now, he took it in both hands and pointed it at me. Dixie came running over to shield me. She pleaded. "What are you doing. This is not going to get you answers. And it sure as chicken snot won't help your situation."

Rotgut snarled. "You better move or I will shoot you, too."

I asked, "What makes you think I know anything?"

Rotgut lowered the weapon and raised a single eyebrow. "Jacob steals a large sum of money from me and needs a place to hide. His ex's little town is an ideal spot."

I never heard a chuckle so out of place, but Dixie did let a snicker escape. "Listen, Ginger here wouldn't even take his calls for a month before the meeting. They weren't what you would call friends. Ginger met with him out of necessity, because his company was large enough to keep us supplied when the general store couldn't."

Rotgut barked back. "Why you doing all the talking. What are you her lawyer or something?"

Dixie chuckled a second time. "No, I'm her friend. She helped me when I needed it most – to raise three kids on my own. I owe her everything and can't let you shoot her."

The big moonshiner glared at her. "Then you tell your friend to tell me what she knows about my money and how to find the weasel who stole it. If she doesn't tell me, then you should move or your kids will be motherless." He raised the gun a second time.

I raised my voice. "Stop this madness. I don't know. I can't tell you what I don't know. Why did you give Jacob more than a million dollars anyway?"

Rotgut flinched his head back a bit. "How did you know it was that much?"

"You wouldn't believe me if I told you the truth."

Rotgut went red again and squinted his face. "You tell me how you knew that. Right now! Only Jacob could have told you it was that much."

I felt my body shaking and had no choice. "It's like this. We have a chicken ghost in this pub and sometimes it tells us stuff. One of our neighbors is a medium and she can communicate with spirits, including our chicken. During a vision the chicken ghost showed her a scene in the woods. They saw you near a still, yelling at someone. You said you lost over a million dollars."

Rotgut blinked a number of times. "Have you been spying on me?"

"What? No, I didn't know you existed until Jacob was hurt."

"I did say that to my partner and I did lose that much money, but not all of it was lost to Jacob. The deal with Jacob was only for five hundred thousand."

"I was not aware of that. So where was the rest of it lost?"

"In bribes. To grease the skids for the deal to be approved by state and federal agencies. We needed special licenses to go legal and make some, um..., problems go away. No one but my partner knew it was just over a million."

"I know it seems bizarre, but the medium saw you in a vision talking about it."

Rotgut went red again and bellowed. "You're stalling. That's an absurd story. You took a lucky guess based on what you knew from Jacob. Because you were part of his scam!" He once again raised and pointed the shotgun at me, this time with purpose.

Dixie pressed against my side and put her arm across

my chest. "Stop! We're telling what we know and we're being completely honest with you."

Rotgut lowered his voice and appeared to talk to himself. "I keep asking how things could get worse. And now I have lunatics telling me a chicken ghost told them about a private conversation I had in our secret still location. This qualifies as getting much worse." Then he glared at Dixie and me, hate in his eyes.

Completely out of character, Dixie's voice cracked. "You're making a huge mistake. She is telling you the truth. We have done nothing to you, why are doing this to us?"

"Because you're lying. Tell me where my money is!"

I tried again. "Look, I know they moved Jacob. The police told me that. But they moved him to a secret location to protect him… from you."

"Why did they tell *you* they moved him?"

"Because I told them you were hunting for Jacob. The police thought you were on the run, hiding after the attempt on Jacob's life with the car. They assumed you would be far from here. But I found out different, that you lost a lot of money and it was personal. Then I warned a detective working on the case."

"You? You told the police. Based on what Casper the friendly chicken ghost told you?"

"Kind of. I figured it out after learning about the

broken deal with you, from Star's vision. And it fit like a puzzle piece with the insurance policies taken out by Jacob's boss, Jake Belanger."

"That insect, Jacob, set all this up!"

I tilted my head. "You still don't know, do you?"

"Know what?"

I shook my head. "Sounds like Belanger made Jacob do all the footwork and put him forward as the mastermind of the deal. But it wasn't Jacob, it was Belanger."

"I've known Jake Belanger for years. He would never double cross me. We grew up together. Why would he do something like that?"

"You will have to ask him."

Rotgut's body stiffened. "Maybe I will ask Belanger some other time. But right now I am asking you where my money is and where did they take Jacob. That is what you need to worry about. So what is your silly chicken ghost telling you now."

"I don't hear it talk to me. It's not like that."

Rotgut burst. "Stop! You think I'm stupid. There is no chicken ghost. You are making it up. NOW TELL ME!" He pointed the gun and cocked it. "You have till the count of three. One… two …"

The harrowing sound that came next resembled a

chicken being tortured and it boomed louder than ever before, then the lights flickered. With the distraction, Guardrail jumped from his stool, sprinted over to Dixie and me, and dove in front of us. The shotgun fired and I waited for the searing pain. But it didn't come. I realized instead my pickled egg jar shattering into a million pieces. My gaze returned to see glass showering Rotgut's head and he folded at the mid-section while falling to the floor. As the large moonshiner hit the ground, it revealed Edith standing just behind Rotgut. She held the neck of a broken bottle. Edith was white but managed to say, "I hate wasting good gin on a piece of chicken spit like him."

Lily came rushing over and sat on the unconscious gunman. Lily eyed her sister still holding the remains of the glass vessel. "Well, help me keep him down." She motioned at Edith to sit next to her and looked around the room. "And someone call the police and have them come remove this piece of garbage from our favorite dining room."

Dixie let out a big breath. "I think I need to swear for real. I'll put the ten dollars in the swear jar up front and then just let me get it all out."

I hugged my bartender. "Don't ruin it now by wasting your money. You did great and were real brave. I don't know how to thank you enough."

Guardrail rolled over on his side. "I'm too old for this. Ouch! I hurt something I didn't know I owned."

Dog rushed over and helped his big partner up. "You

old fool. I think you've seen too many movies." Dog struggled to get his big friend back on his feet.

Guardrail stretched over to one side. "Who knew the floor was that hard. But I couldn't let him shoot you. You did nothing to deserve that."

Dog laughed. "That's an oak plank floor. What did you expect, that it would be soft like a feather stuffed pillow?"

I went over to the injured big man and kissed his cheek. "That was real brave. I can't believe you did it, even though I saw it. But thanks."

Dixie asked him, "Do you need a doctor?"

Guardrail nodded no. "I've had worse. I'll be alright."

Dixie chuckled when she saw where the gun blast went. "Well, that's number nine. You really should put up some sort of board to track the number of pickled egg jars that meet their maker in this pub."

Guardrail moaned. "I love the pickled eggs. Why does it always have to be the pickled egg jar?"

We all laughed and waited for Sheriff Morrison and Aunt Mae, who came before Rotgut woke up. Sheriff Morrison laughed at the sight of Lily and Edith sitting on Rotgut. After sizing up the situation, he decided it was best to call the medics in and let them treat and revive the big moonshiner. I had to admit, the visual of two elderly sisters sitting on Rotgut was odd, even for

The Grumpy Chicken. Piper must have agreed because she took her phone out and snapped a few pictures of the scene.

Chapter Seventeen

Dad neatly piled the new t-shirts next to the hats. Along with Star, he developed a line of merchandise featuring our namesake chicken spirit and it was selling well. Initially, Star sold the stuff out of her shop as I didn't see a way to sell clothes, hats, video disks, and glasses in the pub. We had no displays or shelves for something like that. But Dad fixed that, he used the money from the souvenir sales out of Star's store and bought some nice wooden display racks. After a brief discussion, well Bones thought it was an argument, Dad and I agreed upon a spot near the bar, to the rear of the boys' stools at the end of the bar. It was an unused corner anyway, so it works and Dad is happy.

Dixie and I rearranged tables and covered them with tablecloths. We rarely used linen on our old pub tables, but this was what Dad and Star wanted for tonight.

Guardrail and Dog bickered over whether or not anything would happen tonight as they set up Star's large round table. They earlier retrieved it from the new age store and placed it in the spot we sometimes used for Star's band to play. But tonight, she would forgo the music to conduct a seance.

The pub door flew open and Jacob entered with Nicole on his arm. I had to admit, they made a nice couple. He wore a navy blue suit with a silk tie and she wore a black dinner dress. And following close behind,

Detective Eckart closed the door and stopped just a couple of steps inside. The detective tried to dress for the formal dinner, but the well worn hounds-tooth jacket paired with the loosely knotted tie revealed that he was a cop, through and through. They accepted our invitation, and while a tad early, I was ecstatic that they made the drive to be here.

"Hello, I'm so happy you came. Welcome to the, the...I'm not sure what to call it but I think seance is the right word." I would never be comfortable saying we *want* to talk with ghosts inside the pub.

Jacob hung his head. "I'm a bit embarrassed to be here, but happy."

Nicole tapped his arm. "Don't be silly. Belanger tricked you into making the money drop. You had no idea what was going on and were a victim in all this."

Jacob sighed. "I guess. But I feel so stupid that I got duped."

Eckart folded his arms and frowned. "You were a bit of a rube to get played. And you're lucky I was in a good mood and didn't try to think of a way to charge you for being stupid."

Nicole smiled at the detective. "We appreciate your hard work. Jacob would be dead if you didn't do your job so well."

Eckart smiled back at her, then turned his gaze to me. "So this is the famous haunted pub. I thought it would be bigger."

I chuckled. "That's right. You never came here. The one time you were in town you only saw our small police station."

"That's correct. And I think I was more comfortable there. Are you really going to do this?" He studied the place, top to bottom.

"Yep. A deal is a deal. I told Star we would do a private session and see what happens as thanks for help in the case."

"I have to meet this Star. I've heard of psychics helping the police in cases before, but this is the first time it's happened to one of my cases. I can't tell you how much the boys are ribbing me over it."

Aunt Mae folded cloth napkins with the Sheriff and chimed in while she worked. "Ah, you seem like a tough guy. I think you can handle it."

"I was lucky that I tracked down Belanger through his cell phone use. Some old-fashioned police work. It was my only saving grace. If this see-through chicken of yours found Belanger, too, I would have had to retire. We also picked up Chris Brown and he sang like a canary. But I was happy to get Rotgut off the streets."

I laughed out loud. "An arrest of Rotgut is good anyway you get it, in my book. That is one man that belongs behind bars. If the grumpy chicken helped, so be it. But Belanger and Brown was all yours."

Piper was wiping silverware. "Detective Eckart. I so wanted to meet you. Ginger made it sound like you would be wearing a black helmet."

He scowled at her. "Well, I thought she would be wearing my cuffs the first time I met her. I guess that makes us even."

Dad went over to the detective and shook his hand. "I'm Tom. Ginger's father. I want to thank you for helping us. But I wish you arrested this Rotgut character before he waved a gun at my daughter."

The detective pinched his eyebrows. "To be honest, so do I. I hate when good people are put in harms way. But from what I hear, the bad guy didn't stand a chance."

Dad laughed. "Not in here. This is our turf and we have our ways."

Dixie hollered from the bar. "Even if we told you, you wouldn't believe the way things happen in here. Our stinking feathered phantom defies explanation."

Lily and Edith were sipping tea at their table. We set their table up first as they insisted on serving Earl Grey tea as the guests arrived since Lily thought it was classy. Lily turned to the detective. "It was my sister that brought that Rotbutt guy down. Used a bottle of gin to knock him out. Then me and Edith sat on him to keep him down while we waited for the cops."

Digger sat at the bar, on his stool, drinking a cold beer. He corrected, "Lily, you can't hold down an unconscious man. There was no need, he was knocked out cold. Even after the medics arrived, it took them a while to revive him."

Lily huffed. "Oh, phooey, you're just jealous it was us and not you."

The banter continued and we finished our preparations. Once everything was ready, we sat Jacob and Nicole, along with Detective Eckart, Aunt Mae, and Sheriff Morrison, at a special table in front of the crowd as our honored guests. The rest of the gang took seats and Bones brought out the food. We pulled out all the stops. The meal started with a nice shrimp cocktail and salad followed by Steamship round, baked cod, roasted potatoes, grilled veggies, and rice pilaf. I made it a point to make this meal and without using the grill. The flat-top grill cooked most of the food served to our customers and that works well for our business. But for this meal I wanted it to be more homey and feel formal. Eliminating the grill was symbolic that this was not pub fare. Bones agreed and jumped at the challenge and he hit a home run. The food was excellent.

Dessert was strawberry shortcake because Edith and Lily insisted on it. Just like the odd Earl Grey tea drinking show, they thought formal meals ended with strawberry shortcake. It was not worth upsetting them, so I gave in even though strawberries were out of season.

After we we finished eating, coffee was served and Ida, with Piper's help, set up a camera to record the main event. Star took her position at the head of the large round table covered with black cloth and in the middle sat her crystal ball. "Ginger, Dixie, could you please join me. I would like to start with an exercise to warm things up. A kind of demonstration. The two of you have strong auras that are apt to attract a spirit." Star slid her glass globe closer so it was directly in front of her while we took seats on either side of her. "Ladies, if you could take my hands. I will ask some simple questions and you need to clear your minds. Think of only the grumpy chicken."

Star closed her eyes and took a couple of deep breaths. Then she stared into the globe in front of her. "Are there any benevolent spirits here that would like to communicate?" The crystal ball glowed in two pulses. Star tilted her head. "That's odd. Once means yes, twice means no. I can feel them. Let's try this." She paused a moment, then again closed her eyes and tilted her head. "Please be so kind and let us know, are any spirits present?" The globe flashed once, signaling yes.

Dixie pulled her hand back. "No way! I'm not doing this anymore. It's too freaky."

Star smiled at her. "It's alright. The spirits are comfortable with you. They are present but not talkative right now. We have to be patient. Go on, take my hand." After Dixie complied, Star continued, "Thank you for responding. Could you tell me if you are the chicken spirit that lives in this pub?" The glass ball flashed twice – no. Then Star asked, "Is the chicken spirit here with us?" One flash of light indicated yes.

I pulled my hands back, completely off the table. "What does that mean?

Star wrinkled her forehead. "I think the chicken spirit is here, but doesn't want to talk to a crowd."

Dixie shot back. "Then who's answering our questions?"

Star smiled at Dixie. "Good question, lets see if we can find out. Close your eyes and concentrate real hard, on the chicken" We complied and she continued, "Are you benevolent?" The ball flashed once and Star replied to the crystal object. "Thank you. We're always happy to speak with friends." Star looked to the group. "Maybe it's time to conduct the actual seance. Let's see if we can communicate with this friendly spirit and learn more."

Star asked Piper, Guardrail, Digger, Dad, Edith, Bones and Nicole to join us. They moved to the big round table, which made it crowded. I asked, "Why did you pick people like that?"

Star grinned. "Same as the demonstration. Some people have better auras. And the table is too small to have everyone sit in on the seance."

Dad grumbled. "I didn't even know I had an aura."

Star ignored him and produced some candles, setting them on the table, then lighting the wicks. "Can we get a basket of bread for this table?"

"Bread, what's that for?" Bones responded reflexively when he heard anything sounded like an order for food.

"To attract the spirits." Star moved with an odd grace as she rearranged the candles and crystal ball, then took the bread from Dog Breath. Once she was satisfied with the placement of items on the surface, she asked, "Can someone please turn off the lights. And if you could all hold hands."

Star closed her eyes and tilted her head back. Dog turned the lights off and we waited in candlelight, for what felt like an hour. But after a while, Star sat up straight and started asking questions. After a number of queries, not much happened till Star asked about the grumpy chicken. With that question, three things occurred. First, unassisted the lights turned on. Second, the globe flashed far more than two times. And third, I heard glass clinking, like it was knocked into by a hard object. I looked to bar, the source of the sound, and saw the new pickled egg jar wobble, just a little.

Dixie freaked and jumped back from the table. That ended the séance. I followed suit and left to examine the pickled egg jar. I got up close to it and scrutinized the area. Everything seemed normal and I couldn't explain what caused it to wobble.

Then I saw it, a reflection. It was a transparent chicken hovering over the remains of the séance. Just like Star described, the grumper had white feathers with black and red accents. But I also saw something new. It was a shackle around its left leg. I could see why it limped. It was because of the constraint. I froze and felt all the air leave my body and the reflected image faded away.

I almost missed the commotion as everyone tried to help Star. She crumbled into her chair and blacked out while I was at the bar examining the pickled eggs jar. It was for only a brief moment and I rushed over to help. Star opened her eyes and looked deep into my soul. She said, "It wants to tell you something. But you, and you alone."

Detective Eckart popped like a Jack-in-the-box from his seat next to Jacob and bellowed. "That's it. Parlor games are over. It's time for us to be heading back to Savannah anyway. I hope you all had fun."

Dixie spoke over the detective. "I'm so done with this freaking chicken. It's time for a drink."

Dog Breath nodded. "I think it's time to break out the peach pie. We all could use a good jolt."

Guardrail chuckled. "I have no idea what is going on here. But good idea, partner, I could use a stiff one."

Piper and Ida sprinted to the cameras to see if they recorded everything. I glanced at them and Ida gave me the thumbs up to indicate it was all good. They successfully captured the event.

I spun to speak to Eckart. "So, you got a dose of The Grumpy Chicken. What do you think?"

"I think you're all off your rocker!"

I laughed. "Exactly the answer I expected."

He shook my hand and smiled. "I hope to see you again. But do me a favor, don't invite me to anymore of your dinners."

"I hope to see you again, too, Mr. Vader." He turned and looked for Nicole and Jacob, his ride home.

I went over to Dad who was smiling, too much. "What are you so giddy about."

Dad put his arm around me. "Well, good food and drink always puts me in a fine mood. And I can see you are starting to understand our grumper."

Dixie tried to cut in. "Is it alright to break out the secret stash?"

Dad huffed. "How long you have you worked here. Take care of it. Can't you see I'm having a moment with my daughter?"

Dixie threw her hands in the air and moaned. "Well, Tom is back to normal after all this."

I laughed. After the events of the last year, I was no longer sure what normal meant. And that certainly included tonight's spectacle. But I still had my friends and family and that was all the normal anyone needed. Even if it did mean dealing with a ghost chicken. I could live with that.

Thanks for reading! I hope you enjoyed the book and it would mean so much to me if you could leave a review. Reviews help authors gain more exposure and keep us writing your favorite stories.

You can find all of my books by visiting my Author Page.

Sign up for Constance Barker's New Releases Newsletter where you can find out when my next book is coming out and for special discounted pricing.

I never share or sell your email.

Visit me on Facebook and give me feedback on the characters and their stories.

Catalog of Books

The Chronicles of Agnes Astor Smith

The Peculiar Case of Agnes Astor Smith

The Peculiar Case of the Red Tide

The Grumpy Chicken Irish Pub Series

A Frosty Mug of Murder

Treachery on Tap

Old School Diner Cozy Mysteries

Murder at Stake

Murder Well Done

A Side Order of Deception

Murder, Basted and Barbecued

The Curiosity Shop Cozy Mysteries

The Curious Case of the Cursed Spectacles

The Curious Case of the Cursed Dice

The Curious Case of the Cursed Dagger

The Curious Case of the Cursed Looking Glass

The We're Not Dead Yet Club

Fetch a Pail of Murder

Wedding Bells and Death Knells

Murder or Bust

Pinched, Pilfered and a Pitchfork

A Hot Spot of Murder

Witchy Women of Coven Grove Series

A Hair Raising Blowout

Wash, Rinse, Die

Holiday Hooligans

Color Me Dead

False Nails & Tall Tales

Caesar's Creek Series

A Frozen Scoop of Murder (Caesars Creek Mystery Series Book One)

Death by Chocolate Sundae (Caesars Creek Mystery Series Book Two)

Soft Serve Secrets (Caesars Creek Mystery Series Book Three)

Ice Cream You Scream (Caesars Creek Mystery Series Book Four)

Double Dip Dilemma (Caesars Creek Mystery Series Book Five)

Melted Memories (Caesars Creek Mystery Series Book Six)

Triple Dip Debacle(Caesars Creek Mystery Series Book Seven)

Whipped Wedding Woes(Caesars Creek Mystery Series Book Eight)

A Sprinkle of Tropical Trouble(Caesars Creek Mystery Series Book Nine)

A Drizzle of Deception(Caesars Creek Mystery Series Book Ten)

Sweet Home Mystery Series

Creamed at the Coffee Cabana (Sweet Home Mystery Series Book One)

A Caffeinated Crunch (Sweet Home Mystery Series Book Two)

A Frothy Fiasco (Sweet Home Mystery Series Book Three)

Punked by the Pumpkin(Sweet Home Mystery Series Book Four)

Peppermint Pandemonium(Sweet Home Mystery Series Book Five)

Expresso Messo(Sweet Home Mystery Series Book Six)

A Cuppa Cruise Conundrum(Sweet Home Mystery Series Book Seven)

The Brewing Bride(Sweet Home Mystery Series Book Eight)

Whispering Pines Mystery Series

A Sinister Slice of Murder

Sanctum of Shadows (Whispering Pines Mystery Series)

Curse of the Bloodstone Arrow (Whispering Pines Mystery Series)

Fright Night at the Haunted Inn (Whispering Pines Mystery Series)

Mad River Mystery Series

A Wicked Whack

A Prickly Predicament

A Malevolent Menace

Printed in Great Britain
by Amazon

65920932R00104